TROUBLED GRAVES

LANTERN BEACH EXPOSURE
BOOK 4

CHRISTY BARRITT

CHAPTER
ONE

NOELLE PURDY PAUSED as she walked through the woods. Fear pricked her spine and made the hair on her arms stand on end.

Woods would be an overstatement. Really, the landscape around her was more of a small swath of short and shrubby trees.

They were typical for the coastal climate. Lantern Beach, North Carolina, was basically a sandbar, a stretch of shifting grains with limited vegetation scattered among the many vacation homes and small businesses that had sprung up in recent decades.

None of that really mattered right now.

Only the impending sense of danger did.

Noelle slowly turned her head and glanced behind her.

She saw nothing of concern, nothing that should cause her apprehension.

Still, her heart raced as her synapses fired, indicating a threat could be close.

Noelle had thought being on this trail in the middle of the day should be safe.

All she'd wanted was to clear her head. Being alone in nature usually did the trick.

But now—Noelle couldn't be certain—but she thought someone was behind her.

Following her.

Stalking her?

She swallowed harder.

The sandy path concealed the sound of any footsteps. Most of the growth along the walkway appeared fresh. If it had been winter, the trees and their leaves might have been dry and noisy underfoot.

Not now. In June too much greenery covered the ground.

Nature had created the perfect scenario for someone to follow her in ghostlike silence.

Noelle's throat tightened.

She glanced behind her again but saw no one.

Now she was fully spooked.

She wanted out of these woods.

She hurried across the sandy landscape. The sooner she escaped this area, the better.

Maybe she was being paranoid. So much had happened since Noelle had moved to Lantern Beach to take a position as the lead scientist at the Ocean Essence laboratory. Only a month ago, her mother had disappeared from the memory care facility where she'd been living. They still hadn't found her, and Noelle could only assume the worst.

That fact haunted her every day.

Then at work, it seemed like everyone was on edge—especially after a company board member had been arrested for murder earlier in the year.

Then, just last month, investigators had begun asking questions about a potential chemical dump into the island's waterways. Someone at Ocean Essence was their main suspect—though police still hadn't discovered who.

The company seemed to be hit with problem after problem.

Adding to all that, an uneasy feeling had haunted Noelle for the past couple of days.

She'd tried to ignore it. There was no evidence to prove any of the scenarios popping into her mind were correct.

No one was watching her. Trouble from her past hadn't suddenly reappeared in her life.

Why would it?

So Noelle had dismissed the apprehensive feelings, passing them off for exhaustion. She *had* been working long hours on a new project.

But she couldn't dismiss the sense of foreboding.

At the moment, all she wanted was to get out of these woods. But she couldn't turn around and head back toward her car.

If she did, she'd be walking right into her fears.

If she continued forward, she'd eventually reach the

beach and the vast ocean stretching across the horizon there. This part of the island didn't contain any homes since it was preserved as part of the national seashore and officially part of the property around the historic lighthouse.

At least in the woods the trees provided cover. Out on the shore, Noelle would be completely exposed.

Her heart pulsed faster at the thought.

She should have simply stayed inside today with a good book. But doing so would have reminded her of how alone she was.

She knew it was better that she remained single. But that didn't mean she didn't miss companionship. Having someone in her life who cared about her.

After she and Josh had split, she'd felt such a sense of emptiness.

An ache formed in Noelle's chest at the thought.

She pushed a branch out of her way as her frayed nerves continued to unravel.

Dear Lord, am I in danger? What should I do?

Before she finished her prayer, a noise rattled the brush behind her.

A thrashing sound.

Almost as if something—or someone—were charging toward her.

She glanced over her shoulder.

A man wearing some kind of mask darted onto the pathway.

Noelle screamed when she realized his gaze was on

her. She shouldn't have second-guessed herself moments earlier. Her intuition had been correct.

Someone *was* after her.

She sprinted toward the beach. She had no other choice but to run.

Her next decisions would determine whether or not she escaped . . . and maybe even if she survived.

Noelle felt certain of it.

Just as her feet hit the sandy beach, the man lunged at her. His body collided on top of hers, and she hit the sand.

The air left her lungs as she struggled to breathe under his weight.

This guy was strong and heavy. Noelle couldn't fight him off.

As he pinned her arms behind her, her face pressed into the sand.

She turned her head, panic scrambling through her nerves.

"What do you want from me?" she rushed.

"Everything," the man muttered with a thick accent. "I want everything."

———

As Gunner Mathias walked the shoreline, he frowned and fought the urge to feel sorry for himself.

His current situation wasn't what he'd envisioned for his future.

But life had different plans.

As he took another step across the sand, his body shifted unnaturally. Though the prosthesis on his right leg fit him like a glove, he still resented wearing it. He felt like less of a man with it on.

He took several more steps as he tried to walk off some of his frustrations.

He'd been trained to be a warrior. Warriors didn't feel self-pity. But that was exactly what he'd been feeling lately.

He hoped his time in Lantern Beach would help redirect his thoughts. Would help him refocus and find the joy in life again.

So far, it hadn't.

Maybe that was because no one else could change his thought processes. He was the only one who could do that. Yet, at times, he felt powerless to fight the despair that had been chasing him.

He'd been going through the motions without really living.

He wanted to change that. But how?

Gunner took another step, his leg not moving the way he wanted.

He'd been through intense physical therapy for the past two years.

Those had been some of the hardest months of his life—months he'd endured alone. Family and friends had tried to help, but he'd pushed them away. He didn't need anyone feeling sorry for him.

Gunner mourned for what he'd lost. For what he

had to give up because of that loss. The ripple effects couldn't be counted.

It wasn't only his career he'd lost but also his fiancée. All the future plans they'd made together had vanished, leaving a gap filled with an empty unknown. Maybe he'd even lost his self-respect. Most definitely his purpose.

He knew he could have walked on the beach in front of Hope House, the place where he'd been staying for the past two weeks. The current session at the retreat center had just wrapped up, but he'd decided to stay a little longer.

He hadn't met the goals he'd set before coming, and failure wasn't an option right now. He had to get himself back on track.

The retreat offered counseling, career advisement, and group therapy sessions among other things. All in an idyllic oceanfront setting.

Ty Chambers, a former SEAL who had a heart for helping others recover and reacclimate to civilian life, ran the program.

But Gunner felt the same today as he had when he'd come two weeks ago—not by any fault of Ty's.

Gunner had held himself back. Hadn't opened up the way he should have.

He supposed he didn't want anyone else to see just how much he struggled. Didn't want anyone to feel sorry for him.

He'd been the star quarterback in high school. The leader of his SEAL platoon.

He hated for anyone to see him so . . . so weak.

That was why Gunner had driven to this remote beach on the other end of the island. He'd parked in a public lot and crossed the dune to the nearly private stretch of seashore.

Though they were in the middle of tourist season, no one else was here—just as he'd hoped. His goal was to walk across the beach to the lighthouse.

The hike was especially challenging because of what was known in this area as sugar sand. The fine grains weren't packed hard like the sand on some beaches. Instead, with every step his feet sank and his walk was at least twice as challenging.

On a positive note, the landscape around him was beautiful. The June day couldn't be more gorgeous with its blue sky, low humidity, and comforting breeze.

At one time, Gunner would have looked at this moment and thanked God for his blessings.

But if he were honest with himself, he hadn't been talking to God much lately. Not since his accident.

Maybe one day that would change. Then again, maybe it wouldn't.

He paused as a sound cut through the air.

Was that a . . . scream?

His muscles stiffened. He'd become all too familiar with the sounds of war. Of terror. Of battle.

He could pick them out a mile away.

He knew without a doubt that danger was close. That someone was in trouble.

Gunner picked up his pace as he scanned the landscape around him. But he didn't see anyone or any movements. Only the waves crashing onto the beach and the wind-blown woods beyond that. On the other side of the trees, the lighthouse stood as a beacon for lost travelers.

Had someone nearby been injured?

Sounds could carry across the water, but Gunner couldn't be certain exactly where that cry for help had come from.

That's when he saw a man and a woman tumble from the woods and fall onto the sand.

No, not tumble.

The man had tackled the woman, and she tried to fight him.

She screamed again, clearly in trouble.

She needed help, and God—if He existed—had sent her Gunner? A man without a leg?

He shook off the unwelcome thoughts.

This wasn't the time to feel sorry for himself.

Instead, Gunner would do whatever he could to help her.

With that thought in mind, he yelled, "Hey!"

Then he sprinted across the sand, desperate to reach the woman in time.

NOELLE STRUGGLED against the attacker on top of her.

Fight. Fight with everything you've got inside you. Never give up.

She remembered the words all too well.

They'd been whispered to her when she'd nearly lost her life a little more than two years ago.

With that encouragement in mind, she used her knees. Her arms. Every last ounce of strength inside her to try to get her attacker off.

The man didn't want to kill her. He could have already done that.

Instead, he wanted her for another reason.

That was almost more terrifying.

Noelle let out a guttural yell and tried to push him off again.

The man muttered vulgar insults as he tried to get her under control.

He pinned her again and glared at her, his nostrils flaring.

Then he muttered something in another language.

She froze when she heard his words, and everything went still around her.

What had he said? And why did it sound familiar?

Images of her time in captivity flashed back to her.

The cold, dark room where she'd been imprisoned.

The overwhelming fear and despair that had tried to claim her.

Then . . . a test tube.

A test tube?

Noelle hadn't seen any test tubes when she was being held captive.

Where had that image come from? Wires were getting crossed in her brain.

As quickly as the shock and false memories washed over her, they disappeared.

Her fight for survival surged.

There had to be something she could do!

She wasn't going to let this guy take her anywhere.

Just then, she heard someone yell, "Hey!"

Her attacker jerked his head toward the sound.

Noelle seized the opportunity and grabbed a handful of sand.

She remembered a friend recently telling her a story about how to use sand as a weapon.

As the man turned back toward her, Noelle flung the grains at his face, careful to protect her own eyes.

He howled with pain and loosened his hold on her.

When he did, Noelle twisted and pushed him away.

She scrambled to her feet and ran.

A man on the beach in the distance sprinted toward her.

She didn't hesitate to make a beeline for him.

She didn't know him. Didn't need to.

He appeared strong, capable, and willing to help. That's all she needed to know at the moment.

Noelle didn't look back. She had to put as much distance as possible between herself and her attacker.

She reached the man sprinting toward her on the beach and grabbed his arm. Desperation pulsed through her. "You've got . . . to help me."

Then she turned back toward her attacker.

She blinked as she tried to catch her breath.

The man was gone.

He must have ducked into the woods for cover.

But what was he planning now? Had he left? Or was he circling around only to attack again?

Noelle braced herself, halfway expecting him to reappear closer. To dash out of the woods stronger and more aggressive than before.

She clutched the Good Samaritan's bicep harder and braced herself for what might happen next.

———

The woman's fingers dug into Gunner's skin as he started to go after the man.

But he knew the guy was too far away.

Gunner would never catch up.

Besides, the police were on their way. He'd called them as he ran.

The important thing was that this woman was safe.

However, that didn't mean she was okay.

Gunner glanced at her, his gaze skimming the top of her head as she continued to stare into the woods.

Her hand shook as she shoved it through her light-brown hair. In fact, her entire body trembled.

But he didn't see any visible injuries.

"Did he hurt you?" Tension wavered in his voice as he asked the question.

It was an abomination when men hurt women or children.

He wouldn't stand for it.

"I'm . . . I'm fine." She continued to hold onto Gunner as if he were a shield.

He didn't complain. She could hold onto him all she wanted.

"The police should be here anytime now," Gunner murmured. "Do you know who that guy was? They will want to know everything that just happened."

Finally, the woman glanced up and studied him as if seeing him for the first time.

But the face, half covered with sand, seemed strangely familiar.

Where had he seen this woman before?

Was it . . . ?

His breath caught.

No, it couldn't be.

Gunner shook his head in disbelief.

But he knew she was.

NOELLE GASPED as her mind cleared, and she focused on the man standing in front of her.

The one man she'd never forget.

His face had been forever ingrained in her mind. His hooded gaze. Thick beard. Dark hair. Large, well-defined muscles.

But she *had* to be seeing things.

Because there was no way this man from her dreams was here right now.

Yet he was.

"I've seen you before." A knot formed between his eyes as he studied her.

Noelle's heart nearly pounded out of her rib cage as she continued to stare at his familiar face—a face that swept her back in time.

People said the brain became sharper during tragedy, that details were burned into a person's thoughts.

In her experience, that was true.

She swallowed hard as she tried to figure out what to say. No matter how she looked at this, the situation was surreal.

But she couldn't ignore the facts in front of her. Couldn't ignore how her past and her present had collided.

"You saved me," she muttered.

The man's expression remained stoic, almost stiff. "It looks like you did that yourself. Smart thinking back there with the sand."

The hidden emotion behind the man's gravelly words made it clear there was more to his story.

But what?

Noelle shook her head and realized she wasn't being very clear. "No, I'm not talking about right now. I mean, you saved me in *Moscow*."

His eyes narrowed as he studied her. "You must have me mistaken with someone else."

"No, it was you. I was being held captive with two of my colleagues. SEALs raided the complex where I was being held and swooped us away to safety in a helicopter. You were the one who found me in that cold, horrible room."

The man's eyes widened.

But he didn't say anything. Didn't deny her words.

Even if he did, Noelle knew the truth.

This was the same man who'd rescued her from the hands of truly evil men. She had no doubt about that.

But what was he doing here?

That couldn't be a coincidence, could it?

At the thought, Noelle realized she was gripping his arm as if her life depended on not letting go. Quickly, she dropped her hands from around his bicep. Then she stepped back, nearly tumbling on the uneven sand.

Sirens sounded in the distance, and Noelle knew the police were close.

Still, she didn't know how she and this man—her savior from the past—had ended up here on the same beach at the same time. They were halfway across the world from where they'd last encountered each other. They'd somehow gone from a deserted hospital turned compound in Russia to a remote North Carolina barrier island.

"You being here . . . it's a coincidence?" Noelle stared into his rich brown eyes as she searched for the truth.

The man swallowed hard, appearing for a moment to consider denying her words. Then he shrugged. His deep voice had a soothing effect—just as it had two years ago.

"I never thought we'd cross paths again," he admitted.

She stared at him another moment.

She never thought they'd cross paths either.

She couldn't help but wonder if there was a strange connection between the nightmares she'd left behind in Moscow and the danger she faced today.

Gunner couldn't believe Noelle Purdy stood in front of him.

She'd been part of one of the most daring rescues his SEAL team had ever done.

A rescue that had ultimately ended with him losing his leg just above his knee.

As memories pummeled him, he tried to push them away.

He'd been working with his therapist a long time to try to end the nightmares. To make sure his PTSD didn't worsen and send him spiraling back in time.

But seeing this woman brought everything back.

His head began pulsing as light flashed in his eyes.

At once, Gunner was back on the battlefield. Snow covered the ground, and a cold like he'd never felt before swept around him.

Bombs exploded in the distance. Shouts sounded as men scrambled for their lives.

Fear crackled in the air.

As his vision cleared, Freeman—one of his guys—ran toward a gunman who'd grabbed a civilian woman.

Gunner glanced at the ground in front of his teammate.

Saw the trip line stretched there.

Panic raced through him.

"Stop!" Gunner started to run after him, but it was too late.

An explosion filled the air, sending Gunner toppling backward.

Freeman disappeared into the flames.

Dead.

There was no way his teammate could have survived.

And what about Dreyfus? He was still in that building.

Those thoughts were quickly displaced by the pain ripping through him.

Heat scorched his skin.

The smell of burning flesh drifted up to him.

He tried to stand . . . but he couldn't.

His leg . . . his leg was gone.

Reality hit him—but only for a moment.

Then everything went black.

"Are you okay?" a soft voice pulled him from the flashback.

Gunner snapped back to the present and saw Noelle staring at him with concern.

His head still spun.

His leg ached.

His leg that had been left on the battlefield.

Footsteps rushed behind them.

The police were here.

Just in time . . . because Gunner felt himself spiraling toward the darkest time of his life—a time he was still trying to recover from.

NOELLE WAS RELIEVED when she spotted the police chief and one of her officers jogging toward them.

She ran a hand over her face and felt the grains of sand there. She must be a sight to see. Still, she was simply grateful to be here right now.

That attacker had wanted something from her. If he'd succeeded in taking her with him . . . she couldn't begin to imagine what she might be going through.

She glanced at the man who'd saved her life twice now.

Something flashed in his eyes.

Something haunted. Something almost . . . dangerous.

But what sense did that make?

None.

This man was a hero. The bravest of the brave.

She wouldn't be here today if it weren't for his actions.

She couldn't put her finger on what was going on, and she didn't have time to figure everything out right now.

Instead, Police Chief Cassidy Chambers and Officer Dane Bradshaw paused beside her.

"Noelle," the chief murmured as her gaze scanned both of them. "Gunner. Is everything okay?"

Gunner . . . that was this man's name.

It fit him.

"Noelle?" Cassidy repeated.

Noelle liked the police chief. The two of them went to the same church and had gotten to know each other some through their time there. She knew that Cassidy, as she'd insisted Noelle call her, was tough and determined but also kind and caring.

The woman had to be close to Noelle's age—early thirties—and she was a wife and mom.

"The man ran back into the woods. Since you didn't come across him, he must have cut over in that direction." Noelle pointed toward the lighthouse.

"I'll go check it out." Officer Bradshaw jogged away, gun drawn, and sand flying behind his feet with every pace.

Cassidy turned toward Noelle, tendrils of her blonde hair escaping from the bun she'd pulled it back in. "What happened?"

Noelle gave the police chief an overview of her brief

trek through the woods that had ended with her being attacked.

The chief took notes as Noelle spoke.

The man had said he wanted everything from her.

That was creepy enough.

When Noelle reached the part of the story where the man began speaking in a different language, she hesitated.

Something about his accent . . . she was nearly certain he was Russian.

Hearing that accent had shaken her to the core . . . and she had no idea why. Nor did she know why the image of a test tube had filled her thoughts.

As soon as she'd heard him speak in Russian, it was as if her brain had blipped. Her thoughts had tried to scramble back in time.

Then a stark fear like nothing Noelle had ever known before had consumed her.

She knew deep down inside that whatever was happening was big and serious and deadly.

She knew that it was safer if she kept everything quiet.

She couldn't explain it. Couldn't put her finger on it.

It was simply something she instinctually knew.

As far as Cassidy and Gunner knew, this was a random crime. An attempted robbery or rape.

Nothing else.

Not until Noelle could figure out some things for herself.

"Did you get a good look at this guy's face?" Cassidy observed Noelle as she waited for her response. "Could you see any of his features or what color his eyes were?"

As his image flashed in her mind, she shuddered. "I couldn't tell. He had on one of those creepy pantyhose-over-the-face types of masks."

"I don't see that too often anymore." Cassidy jotted something in her notebook before looking back up at Noelle. "I'm really sorry this happened to you."

"I might have some bruises, but it could have been so much worse." She wiped a hand over her face and felt more gritty grains of sand tumble to the ground.

"Well, I'm glad you're okay." Cassidy turned her gaze to Gunner. "And I'm glad you were here, in the right place at the right time."

Noelle glanced at the man and noted the weariness on his face.

He almost didn't seem like the SEAL who'd rescued her two years ago. That man had been brave, level-headed, and full of life.

This man seemed like a dull reflection of her rescuer.

Why? What had changed?

Was the man she'd seen not real? Had he put on a brave persona for her rescue? She didn't think that was the case.

But something was off right now.

"I'm glad I was here too." Gunner's words sounded as stiff as his motions looked. "But if you don't need anything else from me, I should probably get going . . ."

He shifted on the sand as if he were dealing with some sort of unseen pain.

"Of course," Cassidy said. "I know where to find you if I have any more questions."

Gunner nodded. But as he walked away, Noelle's heart pounded harder. She couldn't just let him leave.

Not when she considered the timing of everything. Their paths had crossed again for a reason . . . right?

She'd always imagined what it would be like to actually see the man who'd rescued her. She'd prayed that she might one day have the opportunity to express her gratitude properly.

But after she'd been whisked away on the helicopter, she hadn't seen him again. He must have escaped on the second helicopter after those explosions had rocked the air.

Noelle was a scientist. She made good money. No doubt it was more than those serving in the military brought home.

It didn't seem right that she was living with many luxuries while the person who'd risked his life to rescue her most likely wasn't.

She turned and called, "Hey, Gunner!"

He paused and pivoted toward her.

"You saved my life," she started before she could second-guess herself. "I never got a chance to say thank you for rescuing me in Moscow."

He shrugged as if it weren't a big deal. "I was just doing my job."

"And today? You stepped in to help me again. Was that part of your job?"

He shook his head. "I was just out for a walk."

"Then let me take you to dinner tonight."

Something washed through his gaze, an emotion Noelle couldn't read.

"Just as a way to say thank you," she clarified. "Nothing else."

Noelle waited for his response, hoping he'd say yes.

Dinner was the least she could do after everything he'd done for her.

She stared up at the man and waited for his answer, hoping he'd let her show her appreciation.

———

Gunner stared at the woman as he considered his response.

Dinner was a nice gesture but a bad idea.

He considered saying yes but only for a moment. Going to eat with this woman would be a mistake for so many reasons.

"Thank you for the offer, but I'm going to have to pass," he finally said. "Besides, you don't owe me anything."

"I know I don't owe you anything." Noelle raised her chin stubbornly. "But you have no idea how many times I thought about what it would be like to show some sort of appreciation to the man who saved me."

Gunner stared at her another moment.

His lips almost wanted to take on a mind of their own, wanted to say yes.

From the moment he'd seen this woman back in Moscow, he'd been attracted to her. There'd been something about the intelligence in her eyes. The strength of her spirit. Her ability to push through her fear . . . she'd left a mark on him.

It didn't hurt that she had light-brown hair that fell to her shoulders in gentle waves, a smile that could light up a room, and eyes that seemed to see into people's souls.

The attraction he'd felt had just been a flash, not something that affected his job. But Gunner had been curious about her since the rescue—curious about what she was doing now, about how she'd healed from her ordeal.

Maybe dinner would be nice.

Then his leg ached again and reminded him that he wasn't the person he'd once been.

No, he was broken—in more ways than one.

Even if it was just a friendly dinner, Gunner should avoid any entanglements and keep things simple. He wasn't in a good place for a relationship yet. He had too much to work on first.

"Thanks again for the invitation, but I'm going to have to decline. I promised Ty we'd go on a long run together." He shrugged. "Anyway, have a good day, ma'am."

Gunner waved to Noelle and then Cassidy.

He needed to get back to Hope House.

But he was glad he'd been at the beach when he was. He hated the thought that something could've happened to Noelle. If he hadn't been there . . . what would that man have done to her? Killed her?

His gut tightened at the thought of her being hurt.

Of anyone else being hurt.

He'd always had a strong sense of justice, and his injury hadn't changed that.

For now, he'd get back to his Jeep and return to Hope House.

Then he'd try to put this entire incident . . . and Noelle Purdy . . . behind him.

CHAPTER
FIVE

CASSIDY CHAMBERS LISTENED to the exchange between Gunner and Noelle and knew she was missing something.

She wanted to know what. Not just out of nosiness either. Maybe there was some kind of hidden link between Gunner's and Noelle's pasts and the assault that had happened here today.

She turned to Noelle and studied her face. "How do you know Gunner?"

Cassidy had met the woman at church, and she seemed nice. Noelle was good friends with Rachel Atwood, another newcomer to the island whom Cassidy had recently gotten to know.

The two women both worked at Ocean Essence, a cosmetics lab that had received a lot of scrutiny since they'd opened a facility on the island not long ago. Lantern Beach wasn't the ideal location for a lab belonging to a world-renowned skincare company.

All kinds of red flags had been raised when they'd established a facility here.

"You're not going to believe me if I tell you." Noelle rubbed her arms and stared into the distance at the ocean as if her mind had been swept back in time.

"Try me."

Noelle let out a long breath, and her gaze suddenly appeared even more burdened.

"The truth is, a little more than two years ago, I was working overseas in France for a different laboratory doing research on various skin diseases," Noelle started. "While I was working late one night, six gunmen breeched the building. They killed five of my colleagues."

Cassidy sucked in a breath. That wasn't what she'd expected. "That's terrible. I'm so sorry."

Noelle continued, a strained look in her eyes. "They took two of my colleagues and me hostage. We were drugged, and when we awoke . . . we discovered we were outside of Moscow in an old hospital. The place was cold. Abandoned. The most frightening place I've ever seen or experienced."

"Russia?" Cassidy's voice climbed with surprise.

"That's right."

"Why Moscow? Why did they abduct you?" The questions raced through Cassidy's mind as she tried to form a picture of what might be going on here.

"I still don't have all the answers. But I know these guys wanted money." Noelle rubbed her throat. "They were asking for millions from the US government in return for my colleagues and me being released unharmed."

Cassidy shifted as she tried to make sense of what Noelle told her. "Why you three?"

Noelle shrugged. "Because we were Americans working for a billion-dollar company, I suppose."

"What did they do to you while you were held captive?"

"They kept us alive. Except for Bartholomew." A knot lodged in her throat. "He didn't come back with us. The pieces have been hard to put together."

Cassidy had heard stories like that before, though they generally seemed to happen in the Middle East. "Did the company or the government pay for your release?"

"No, but they sent the military for us. Thomas and I were held captive for three weeks. On the first day of the fourth week, a team of Navy SEALs rescued us. Gunner was one of them."

Wow. Cassidy couldn't get over Noelle's story . . . or the timing of both Noelle and Gunner being on the island right now.

"I'm so sorry you went through that. I can't even imagine." Compassion flashed in Cassidy's eyes. "Who was responsible?"

"A group of men who call themselves the Alphas. Several of them died during the rescue and the explosion that occurred afterward. But there are more of these guys. I check the news occasionally, looking for any updates on them, just because . . ." She shrugged. "I guess I don't really know why. To confirm that they're no longer a threat, I suppose. So far, that has proven to be the case."

Cassidy didn't bother to hide her disbelief. "And now you and Gunner just happened to run into each other here in Lantern Beach?"

Noelle shrugged, her eyes still dazed. "It's crazy, isn't it?"

Cassidy couldn't help but muse that maybe it wasn't that much of a coincidence after all. Most things happened for a purpose. Maybe there was a reason Noelle and Gunner had encountered each other again here in Lantern Beach.

Maybe they both needed to heal and needed each other to do so.

Cassidy's husband, Ty, ran Hope House.

She'd interacted several times with Gunner since he had arrived two weeks ago—exactly three days after Cassidy and Ty and their young daughter, Faith, had returned from a much-needed Caribbean vacation.

As Cassidy had observed Gunner throughout his stay, she'd seen the brokenness in his gaze.

He was someone who'd always been at the top of his game. But Ty told her that when Gunner lost two members of his team, along with his leg, that his life had taken a turn for the worse, to say the least.

Not only did Gunner feel responsible and guilty for the death of his teammates, but he needed to find a new purpose in life without his career. The loss of his leg had been challenging, a tough pill to swallow, as the saying went. To look at him wearing long pants, someone might not even know he was an amputee. But it was a fact he clearly couldn't forget.

"Anyway . . . is there any reason that I need to stick around here?" Noelle glanced at Cassidy and shivered as if frightened. "Do you have any more questions for me?"

"I think I've got what I need for now. Bradshaw and I are going to search the woods. I'll also keep my eyes open for anyone on the island who's acting suspicious. We need to catch this guy."

It seemed ironic for Cassidy to say that, considering the fact there always seemed to be someone on the island acting suspicious. But she didn't mention that to Noelle. No need to concern her any more than she already was.

"You're free to go." Cassidy nodded reassuringly. "I'll find you if I need you."

Noelle's eyes still looked burdened as she rubbed her arms. "Okay, then. I'll be on my way."

"Do you want me to drive you back to your place?" Cassidy had to wonder if there was something Noelle wasn't telling her. She looked jumpy. Her gaze looked strained. And she almost had an air of nervousness about her.

Classic signs that someone had a secret.

Was this just simply a random crime? It seemed so strange if it was.

And if it wasn't random, then Noelle could be a target again. Cassidy didn't like those implications.

Noelle waved her hand in the air. "I think I was just in the wrong place at the wrong time. I should be fine."

Cassidy stared the woman another moment, giving her a chance to change her mind.

But Noelle didn't alter her statement.

Instead, she turned to head back to her own vehicle.

"I'll walk with you," Cassidy called. "Just to be safe."

Noelle didn't argue.

Cassidy's gaze scanned everything around them as they walked.

Was more trouble brewing on the island?

Her gut instinct told her that was a definite yes.

CHAPTER
SIX

NOELLE SHOULD HAVE LET Cassidy or one of her officers escort her home.

She was on edge for the entire drive back to her cottage. She couldn't stop looking around. She even checked the back seat of her car several times—as if someone might suddenly materialize there.

She knew better.

But her fear was stronger than her logic right now.

She couldn't wait to get home. She'd be safe there.

That was how she felt whenever she was inside the little nine hundred-square-foot cottage she called home.

Despite the decent salary she made, houses on the island were expensive. The closer to the ocean or the newer the house, the more costly.

Noelle had found a little beach box—that's what the squarish homes standing on pilings were called. The roof had needed replacing, and the inside had been outdated. Since Noelle had purchased it, she'd spent much of her free time fixing it up.

She'd painted the orange wood paneling a greenish gray—sea salt, the label said. She'd hired a contractor to install gray wood floors. She'd replaced the countertops and painted the cabinets nautical blue. She was currently working on replacing the ceiling fans and light fixtures.

She still had a lot of work to do, but the place had already been transformed.

Now, the house felt like home. The residence was a block from the ocean, but at night, if Noelle opened her windows, she could hear the waves breaking on the shore. She had one permanent neighbor, and the rest of the houses around her were rentals.

She was simply grateful to have the opportunity to live on this island and get to know the small community here.

Now, all of that seemed at risk.

Especially if trouble from her past had found her here.

She thought she'd left the danger behind. Initially after her rescue, she'd feared those men would find her again as a means of vengeance. But they hadn't.

Things had been relatively peaceful.

Until now.

If it wasn't for the security system she'd installed at her house, she probably wouldn't stay here tonight. She'd most likely call her friend Rachel and see if she could stay there instead.

But if any doors or windows at her place had been opened, Noelle would have gotten a notice on her phone. Plus, she had cameras mounted by her exterior doors, and she'd also get an alert about any movement there.

The added security cost wasn't cheap, but Noelle figured it was worth it if it gave her peace of mind. Especially as a single woman. Especially after what happened in Moscow. Her abduction felt like a permanent scar on her soul, something she thought about every day.

And every day, she was grateful for another chance at life. Thankful to be alive. Thankful because she knew two Navy SEALs had been killed during her rescue but she survived.

She'd heard about their deaths on the news, and it was a sacrifice she'd always remember.

She arrived home without incident and punched in the code to her door ready to go inside and get settled.

A moment later, the lock mechanism churned, and Noelle opened the door.

Her cheerful house greeted her.

Home sweet home.

She never thought she'd be single again. But that had changed when her husband, Josh, had left her for a new life.

From now on, it was the single life for her. She'd moved on and had learned to be content alone. Usually.

Still, the thought of going through the kind of heartache she'd experienced after her divorce again was enough to send her spiraling. Her protective walls were up.

And the walls were permanent.

Noelle left her purse and keys on a bookshelf near the door and headed toward the kitchen. She poured herself a glass of water and quickly drank it, trying to calm her frayed nerves.

It would be a long time before she forgot about what happened today—if ever. Those terrifying moments would be forever ingrained in her head.

Just like when her mom had disappeared.

Just like when Noelle had been abducted.

That's why she had so easily remembered Gunner. His image was indelibly engraved in her mind. He'd represented hope. Represented selflessness. Represented strength.

She remembered how she'd invited Gunner to dinner and his outright rejection of her offer.

Noelle wasn't offended or even insulted.

Well, maybe *a little* insulted.

Had the man thought she was hitting on him?

Then again, maybe he was married or had a girlfriend, and going to dinner with a single woman would have been awkward.

That was probably it.

But Noelle couldn't help but think there was more to his story. More to that haunted look in his eyes and the stiffness in his steps.

Had he been injured since she last saw him? Had the death of his two colleagues changed him?

She set her glass on the counter and turned. Maybe the best thing she could do right now was take a shower. Get this sand off her skin.

Then she could curl up with a book, crack a window open—but only with the safety latches in place—and relax inside the security of her cottage for the rest of the evening.

Tomorrow, she'd head to church. Have lunch with Rachel and Jonah. Then she'd return to the grind on Monday.

She stepped into her room and kicked her shoes off.

As she did, she sensed something behind her.

Movement.

She froze, hoping the stress of the day was just playing with her mind.

But Noelle knew it wasn't.

Before she could react, a figure sprang at her from the shadows.

"You didn't think you'd get away that easily, did you?" he growled. "We have a conversation to finish."

———

Gunner drew in a deep breath of ocean air as he pulled into the driveway at Ty Chambers' house.

He tried to put the incident at the lighthouse beach behind him.

But that was easier said than done.

As he climbed from his Jeep, Kujo—Ty's golden retriever—sashayed over to say hello. Ty followed behind, dressed in running shorts, a T-shirt, and sneakers.

"You're just in time." Ty placed his hands on his hips as he waited. "Ready for our run?"

Gunner paused on the driveway and considered his options. He'd been hoping Ty had forgotten. He wasn't sure he could handle another five-mile run.

"I'm not sure I'm feeling up for a run today."

"Sometimes it's not a matter of feeling up for it. It's a matter of deciding you need to be up for it."

Gunner had always known Ty was a wise man and a good leader. Gunner had worked with Ty on more than one occasion as a Navy SEAL. Everyone had always spoken highly of the man, and that hadn't changed when Ty had gotten out of the military.

However, Gunner wasn't in the mood for one of Ty's inspiring pep talks right now. Not after what had happened. Not after seeing Noelle again had sent his thoughts spiraling.

"The marathon is only two months away," Ty reminded him as the wind blew and tousled Ty's short, light-brown hair. "We don't have any time to waste."

The two of them had registered for a race up in Virginia Beach. Gunner had immediately second-guessed that decision. But he'd already made the commitment and wasn't going to back out.

Besides, Gunner knew his friend's words were true. Two months wasn't long when training for a marathon. They needed to utilize all the free time they had.

"Fine." Gunner nodded at the cabana behind Ty's

house where he'd been staying. "Let me get my shoes on."

He went into the small, coral-colored building and changed into his running shoes.

Instead of running on the sandy beach, the two of them headed to the gravel road.

Ty had also been working with him on the obstacle course at the Blackout Headquarters as Gunner tried to learn to function—and thrive—with his amputated leg.

It had been challenging, disheartening, and downright discouraging at times.

But Ty hadn't let up on him. He insisted that one day, Gunner would thank him.

This part of the island was fairly secluded. He and Ty kept a steady pace as they jogged together, which gave them a good opportunity to talk.

Gunner knew exactly what Ty would bring up. He'd been anticipating it, for that matter. Gunner had no doubt that Ty had talked to Cassidy and knew about the events from earlier today.

Ty glanced at him, barely breaking a sweat. "So, what happened by the lighthouse earlier?"

And there it was.

There was no need to delay the inevitable.

Not if he wanted to heal. That's what Ty would say.

Gunner gave Ty the short version of what had unfolded on the secluded beach earlier.

"So Noelle is the woman you rescued in Moscow? And you two just happened to run into each other on Lantern Beach?" Ty glanced at Gunner, his eyes narrowed with surprise and his voice containing an almost dubious tone.

"Crazy, isn't it?" Gunner continued to stride forward. Over the past couple of weeks of running with Ty, he'd grown more accustomed to running with his prosthetic. He wasn't sure he'd ever fully get used to it, however.

"I'd say so. I know that has to be tough for you. Her rescue mission was the one that changed everything." Ty's last sentence came out quieter than the first—quieter because of the life-altering seriousness of that moment.

"You can say that again." Gunner's voice cracked as he said the words.

"You do know it's not your fault what happened." Ty's tone dipped even lower.

Gunner's throat tightened as familiar guilt began to pummel him. The emotion seemed like a constant companion lately. "It feels like my fault."

"We can't always trust our feelings."

"You're really good at this pep talk thing, you know?" Yes, Gunner was trying to deflect, and he had no shame in that.

Ty let out a chuckle. "I try."

They paced side by side for several minutes in silence. As the sun beat down on them, Gunner's thoughts wandered back to Noelle.

He still couldn't believe the two of them had run into each other again.

If Gunner believed God actually cared, then maybe

he'd think that he and Noelle had been brought back together for a purpose. But maybe thinking that way was naive. He wasn't sure.

He'd thought about Noelle often since her rescue. There had been something different about her. She'd been terrified yet had a fiery determination to survive.

But Gunner knew the situation had taken a toll on her.

He'd wondered how she recovered after what she'd been through.

When he remembered her attack today, his muscles tightened again.

She deserved better. She deserved to feel safe and protected.

He only hoped Cassidy was able to catch the man who'd attacked her.

CHAPTER
SEVEN

A RUSH of adrenaline surged through Noelle as her survival instincts kicked in.

The man shoved her to the floor.

Then he was on top of her.

His hands went to her throat, and he squeezed until Noelle couldn't breathe.

She swung her arms as she fought to get him off. As she fought to force air into her lungs.

Her efforts did no good.

"Stop trying." A thick Russian accent filled the man's words, almost as if he'd tried to conceal his accent but couldn't any longer. "You won't beat me."

Noelle knew he spoke the truth. But she continued to fight him until she'd exhausted herself.

Finally, she grew still and waited for whatever he would do next.

Her heart pounded in her ears as fear whipped through her.

"We need something from you." He stared down at her, wearing that same pantyhose mask that concealed his features. "I think you know what. You need to come with me."

Images of that test tube filled her thoughts again.

Along with new images. One of a lab coat. Another of some equipment.

And Bartholomew being killed in front of her eyes.

She gasped as her mind reeled back in time.

No . . . she hadn't seen her colleague die.

Then why did she feel like a memory was fighting to surface? What sense did any of this make? He'd been killed in his prison cell, not in front of her.

The man loosened his grip on her throat enough for her to say, "I'll never help you. Never!"

He sneered. "We figured you might say that. That's why we had to take these drastic measures."

Drastic measures? What did that mean?

Noelle's heart pounded harder as she waited for him to continue.

"The time is right now. You're coming with me." He started to pull her from the floor.

She jerked back. "You'll have to kill me first."

"You won't be any good to us dead."

Another shock of fear raced through her, and she thrashed again. "Get off of me, you monster!"

Rage seemed to fill him, and he began to punch her. Again. And again. And again.

Then sirens sounded in the distance.

Sirens?

Had someone called the police?

He heard them too. Panic raced through his gaze.

He stared at Noelle, regret seeming to wash over him.

He hadn't meant to beat her, had he? Rage had kicked in. He'd flown off the handle. Become uncontrolled. Shown his desperation.

"I can't finish this now," he muttered. Then, still straddled on top of her, he pulled out his phone. He punched the screen and showed it to Noelle.

She gasped when she saw the image of her mother there . . . her mother in a rocking chair outside a house Noelle had never seen before.

Her mother . . . the one who'd been missing for the past month. Who'd had dementia and wandered away from the facility where she'd lived.

She still hadn't been found, and Noelle had assumed the worst . . .

Tears filled her eyes.

"You have my mom?" Her words sounded rasped as they left her lips. "Where is she?"

"That's not important. Not right now. Just know, if you don't comply with what we tell you, she'll die."

"But . . ." Noelle's thoughts scrambled to make sense of the situation.

"I'll be back. I promise you that. If you do anything to ruin our plan, we'll kill her. That includes you telling the cops. Understand?"

She nodded, feeling helpless to do anything as fear rolled through her.

Then the man rammed his fist into the side of her face again.

"Just so you'll know how your mom will suffer if you don't comply," he whispered.

Her head spun until she nearly passed out.

As the sirens got louder, the man rose, cast her a dismissive glance, and stepped toward the door.

"We'll know if you tell anyone," he muttered as he stared back at her. "Take my word for it."

Then he was gone.

Noelle moaned as she rolled over on the floor.

Then she pushed herself upright.

Fight. Fight with everything you've got inside you. Never give up.

She had to call for help. Whether or not she would report the man, she didn't know.

But if she didn't get help, then she could be in serious trouble.

She already felt her face swelling. Felt the blood trickling from her lips. Her head spinning. Her vision blurring.

Using her last ounce of energy, she crawled across the floor, ribs aching at the motion. Then she reached as far as she could and grabbed the cell phone she'd left on her dresser.

Immediately afterward, she collapsed back onto the floor.

The last thing Noelle managed to push herself to do was to dial 911.

Gunner took another bite of his crisp apple.

He'd already showered and changed after his run with Ty. Then he'd grabbed an apple and stepped outside to enjoy more of the day.

In the distance, he spotted Ty throwing a frisbee with Kujo on the shore.

He started over the dune to join them when Cassidy walked over from the house next door—Ty's parents' place.

She offered a bright smile as she called, "Hey, Gunner."

She held her daughter, Faith, in her arms. The girl was twenty months old and adorable with her blonde hair and bright eyes. She was clearly her parents' pride and joy.

Just then, Ty emerged from the other side of the dune and greeted her, Kujo on his heels. He took Faith from Cassidy, talking baby gibberish, as Gunner always called it, before kissing the girl's cheeks.

The sight of the three of them together did something strange to Gunner's heart. Made it ache uncontrollably.

This was what he wanted—what Ty had.

At least, Gunner *had* wanted it at one time.

He'd dreamed about having a family of his own.

But all those hopes had disappeared when his life had been turned upside down.

Even though Gunner had been engaged to Laura

Swenson during his last mission, he'd broken up with her not long afterward. There was no need to make her endure everything he was going through, for her to carry his burden.

Laura had insisted she wanted to be with him. For a long time, she'd even come to the hospital to try to convince him of her faithfulness and dedication.

But Gunner had driven her away. He'd gotten mean. Told her he didn't love her.

When she'd cried, he'd almost broken down. He'd almost told her the truth.

But he hadn't.

The last he'd heard, Laura was now engaged to someone else. Gunner was happy for her. She deserved the best.

And Gunner was no longer that.

As he, Ty, and Cassidy all stood beneath the house making small talk, Cassidy's phone rang, and she placed it to her ear. Only a few seconds into the conversation, her smile disappeared. She paced away as she muttered several things to the person on the other line.

What was that about? Gunner wondered.

Finally, Cassidy ended the call and turned back to Ty with a frown on her face. "That was Paige at dispatch. Noelle was just attacked in her home."

Gunner's heart pounded faster. "What?"

He knew he wasn't supposed to be part of this conversation. But he couldn't ignore what Cassidy had just said.

"Apparently, a man was waiting inside her home

when she arrived. She's pretty beaten up. She's headed to the clinic now." Cassidy slid her phone back into her pocket and frowned.

A new round of guilt filled Gunner.

If he'd agreed to go to dinner with her, would any of this have happened?

Maybe not.

It had to be the same guy who'd attacked her earlier.

"I'm going to get down there so I can question her myself." Cassidy squeezed Faith's hand as she softened her voice. "I promise I'll be back tonight to tuck you in."

"Do what you have to do," Ty said. "Faith and I will be fine."

Gunner wasn't sure what he was doing when he stepped forward, but he couldn't just stay here. "Any chance I can go with you?"

Where had that question come from? He wasn't even sure. But now it was out there, and he couldn't take it back.

Cassidy studied him a moment as if evaluating his mental state or motives. Finally, she nodded. "You can come to the clinic with me, but I make no promises about seeing Noelle. That will be up to her."

"Of course." Gunner had no idea what he might accomplish by going to the clinic.

But somehow, he felt as if he'd let Noelle down earlier. He wanted to make it up to her. to ensure she was safe.

Who could have done something like this to her?

Why would anyone want to hurt someone as kind as she was?

A new sense of determination rose in him.

Maybe he should make it his mission to find out.

Besides . . . this was the first time in a long time he'd felt both purpose and passion rise up in him.

The only comfort he'd had after his last mission was the realization that Noelle and her colleague were safe.

He couldn't let that be ruined.

NOELLE'S HEAD THROBBED UNCONTROLLABLY. Her face ached.

The doctor had assured her that her jaw wasn't broken, but it felt that way.

She was still amazed that man hadn't killed her. Yet she knew he'd be back.

He'd told her she needed to comply.

Which made her feel as if there was some type of other plan in place.

A bigger plan.

A deadly plan.

For that reason, she almost wished he had just taken her life. It would probably be less painful than what he wanted from her.

He'd said she needed to finish what she'd started.

She had no idea what that even meant.

But based on the evil tone of his voice, it wasn't good.

She couldn't do what he'd asked her to do.

What he'd demanded.

She just couldn't.

Yet if she didn't . . . she remembered that picture of her mom.

Tears rushed to her eyes.

Noelle was in an impossible situation.

Her mom was alive . . . yet still so far out of reach.

Doc Clemson wanted to keep her overnight for observation, especially since Noelle had hit her head when the man knocked her to the floor.

That was fine by her. She didn't want to go back to her house and be there by herself. She knew she could call Rachel, but she really didn't want everyone to know about this. Didn't want to have to answer questions.

However, the thought was illogical because as soon as anyone took a look at her face, they'd know something bad had happened. No amount of makeup could cover up these wounds.

Heaviness pressed on Noelle at the thought.

A knock sounded at her door, and she called, "Come in."

Cassidy stepped inside.

"Hey, Noelle . . . I'm so sorry to hear what happened." Compassion rang through the police chief's voice as she paused by Noelle's bedside.

"I guess I should have had you escort me home after all." Noelle offered a weak smile.

"Do you want to tell me what happened?" Cassidy

stared down at her, not a hint of amusement in her gaze after Noelle's off-the-wall comment.

She ran through the story with Cassidy . . . most of it. The physical parts of it.

She couldn't tell Cassidy all the details of the conversation . . . not if she wanted her mom to live.

Nausea gurgled inside her at the thought.

"And you have no idea who this man was?" Cassidy narrowed her eyes as she studied Noelle.

Noelle shook her head, trying to push away her guilt. She knew she should tell Cassidy about the images flashing in her head. But she couldn't. She just couldn't. She had no idea what they meant or if they were even relevant.

"I don't know who he was." Her throat burned as she said the words. "I've never seen him before today."

Cassidy paused and shifted. "Maybe this is a crazy question but . . . you don't think this has anything to do with your abduction two years ago, do you?"

Noelle's throat tightened. "I don't think so. I mean, I don't know why those men would come all this way for me. Not when there are other people a lot closer to them that they could grab and hold hostage. There's nothing special about me."

"You were once a leading doctor for infectious diseases. That sounds like reason enough, don't you think?"

"They abducted me before, only to lock me in a room. I'm just not sure."

Cassidy's gaze remained assessing as she nodded.

"I'm going to have one of my officers remain here at the clinic, just to be sure you're safe."

Noelle hated for people to make a big deal about her, but she'd feel better knowing someone was standing guard.

She needed time to figure things out. Because that man would be back. She was sure of it.

Cassidy stepped toward the door and paused. "By the way, Gunner was near me when I got the call about you and asked if he could come to the clinic. I told him I wasn't sure if you would want to see him or not, however. What should I tell him? It's your call."

Gunner? He'd come to see her?

Shock coursed through Noelle, especially when she considered how earlier he'd acted like he wanted nothing to do with her.

Noelle thought about it only a moment before nodding. If what was happening did somehow have a tie with her abduction, then Gunner might be able to help her find answers.

"Send him in," she said.

Cassidy nodded before exiting the room. A few moments later, Gunner's familiar face appeared in the doorway. His dark beard fit him, giving him a strong, distinguished look. But his eyes . . . they were so haunted.

She wanted to dive into them and dig up whatever ghosts had caused the look. That thought was danger-ous, however. Just because the man had saved her didn't mean he was her savior.

After her rescue two years ago, Noelle had thought about Gunner a lot—and not just because of the unwavering gratitude she felt toward him.

He'd become somewhat of a superhero in her mind, she supposed. There had even been times after her breakup with Josh when Noelle had wondered what it would be like to date someone like Gunner. Someone who wasn't afraid to face the hard stuff with her.

But something about Gunner had changed since the day he'd rescued her. Noelle couldn't help but be curious about what exactly it was.

"Hey." He paused awkwardly near her bed, not getting too close.

"Hey," she echoed.

He shifted again as if he didn't know exactly how to start. "I'm sorry about what happened today."

"It's not your fault."

"I can't help but think I should've taken you up on that offer to go to dinner together." His voice cracked. "Maybe this wouldn't have happened."

"Who's to say the guy wouldn't have been waiting for me afterward?" Her question lingered in the air.

But both of them already knew the answer.

He would have been.

Events had been set into motion . . . events that Noelle might be powerless to stop.

———

Gunner swallowed as he tried to figure out exactly what he wanted to say. Noelle had made a good point. She would have been vulnerable either way.

But that still didn't mean he liked it.

Why *had* he come here anyway? He wasn't exactly sure. He'd only known that he wanted to see her. *Needed* to see her.

The only comfort he'd gotten out of that last mission was in knowing Noelle and her colleague were safe.

The thought of something happening to Noelle now after everything she'd been through—everything she and Gunner had both been through—seemed like such a shame.

How did Gunner tell her that?

He couldn't. Not without overexplaining. And he didn't want to do that.

Yet another part of him had wanted to see her with his own eyes. To know that she was okay.

He'd even come to this clinic to do so.

Ever since he'd lost his leg, he'd hated any type of medical facility. The mere smell of them sent his mind reeling back in time.

"I appreciate the fact you wanted to check on me," Noelle murmured, her gaze smoky with emotion. "But please, don't feel guilty. The only one at fault here is the man who did this to me."

Gunner stepped closer, his thoughts turning from his guilt to the reality of what had happened. That was what his therapist had told him to do. To focus on the tangible things.

Looking at the facts grounded him in reality.

"I take it you don't know who that man was?" His voice came out hoarse.

Noelle shook her head as a shadow filled her gaze. "I've never seen him before today."

"And he didn't say anything that might give you a clue as to what he wanted? If he didn't kill you, then he wanted . . . something." Gunner felt himself switching into SEAL mode—even though he was officially no longer in the military.

He watched as Noelle swallowed hard.

She was hiding something, wasn't she?

Gunner was trained in interrogation techniques. He could tell when someone was lying.

But what in the world would Noelle have to hide?

He didn't know. But he reminded himself to be cautious. Especially when he remembered his theory that someone on that last mission had been a mole. It was the only way the Alphas could have known his team was coming and set them up to fail.

Did Noelle know anything about that?

"I don't know," Noelle finally said with an unconvincing shrug. "Your guess is as good as mine."

Gunner's mind drifted back to the details of the rescue. Some of the particulars were on a need-to-know basis. His team's mission had been strictly tactical. That meant he hadn't needed to know all the specifics about the events leading up to the rescue. He only needed to know as much as necessary to perform his operation.

But what if there was something more that Gunner needed to know now?

If so, how would he find out that information? He could call his former commander. Maybe Commander Ford would share details.

But should Gunner take things that far? Probably not.

He should just let this be.

He rolled his shoulders back as he tried to process his thoughts.

He'd come to Hope House to heal.

But what if part of the healing process involved making peace with that final mission and how it had torn his life apart?

And maybe even to secure the legacy of that rescue by ensuring that Noelle Purdy remained safe?

NOELLE COULD SEE Gunner was thinking about something that he wasn't saying aloud.

Did he suspect that she was hiding information? She couldn't tell anyone about her mother's abduction.

The man didn't know her well enough to read that on her expression, did he?

She wasn't sure. But right now, she almost felt as if the man could see right through her.

Memories of her time in that dark, cold room tried to surface. It was almost as if there were part of her captivity that had remained buried in the recesses of her mind.

But what sense did that make? She remembered plenty about that time. About the room she'd been kept in. The terrible meals she'd been fed—when she'd been fed at all.

The rats that came out at night to scamper around her.

Noelle had been afraid the creatures were so hungry that they might try to eat her.

Irrational maybe. But the fear had been real at the time.

No one had ever suggested to her that she had amnesia.

Nothing was making sense.

But her questions felt like a burden she was ill-equipped to carry.

Why couldn't she go back to the old days, back to when she'd been carefree and innocent? Back to when she'd wanted to be a scientist and a mom. Back to when she'd wanted to take family vacations and make happy memories she could reminiscence about one day.

Nothing had worked out the way she planned.

Her abduction had changed her—and not in good ways. But it wasn't the only thing that had altered her. Hard times seemed a permanent part of her life.

Her throat burned as she pushed the memories away.

Finally, Gunner took a step back. "I should let you rest. I just felt compelled to come talk to you myself. I hope I didn't overstep."

"I understand." The rescue had bonded them in some abstract way. Noelle wondered if that was typical in these situations.

She didn't know, but she would guess that to be true.

Gunner had been so strong and encouraging. She'd never met anyone like him before.

Fight. Fight with everything you've got inside you. Never give up.

She could still hear him saying those words. She still repeated them whenever times got tough.

Noelle couldn't get over the fact that somehow their lives had been drawn together again.

Gunner started out of the room but then paused. He turned toward her, something about his gait different.

Noelle hadn't noticed it before. Probably because she'd been too distracted with everything else that had happened today.

Had he injured himself? Hurt his knee or hip maybe?

It was hard to say. He wore jeans and sneakers, and any injuries weren't visible. She only noticed his gait had changed.

"If you don't mind, I'd like to give you my phone number," he murmured. "And if you need anything, I want you to let me know."

The offer was touching, despite his gruff manner.

"I'm sure you didn't come here to the island to keep an eye on me. That wouldn't really be fair to you now, would it?" Noelle tried her best not to depend on others —though sometimes it was impossible. Still, she couldn't allow him to babysit her.

"I'd actually feel a lot better if I knew how you were doing. It would not only help you, but it would also help me. So really, the request is selfish."

Noelle let out a chuckle at his attempt to rationalize his request.

But as he found a pad of paper and pen, Noelle gave him her number, and he gave her his.

Then, with one more glance from those hooded eyes, he left.

The whole situation had her curious.

There was more to Gunner's story. She was sure of it.

She tried not to think about it.

Despite her resolve, questions continued to pummel her mind.

———

Gunner didn't want to leave the clinic—which was why he'd told Cassidy he would stay and catch a ride home later.

He knew his choice didn't make sense. Other than his and Noelle's connection from the past, he had no reason to stay with this woman.

Yet he somehow felt the unexplainable need to protect her. He'd done it once.

And he'd lost his leg as a result.

Gunner didn't resent Noelle for what had happened. But to see her suffer now after everything he'd lost seemed a shame. Something good *had* to come from that mission.

That good thing had always been Noelle.

The woman was smart. Some people had even said she was brilliant. One of the brightest minds of this decade, as one of her coworkers had been quoted saying.

And Gunner had always believed good could come from his sacrifice. Good in the form of Noelle and the medical contributions she might make to the world at large.

So why was someone targeting her now?

He paced outside the door to her room at the clinic.

He would be imposing if he stayed in her room. But he could somehow keep guard outside. He had to do *something* to help. An unseen compulsion gripped him.

"How's it going, man?" a deep voice said behind him.

He glanced back and saw Braden Dillinger, another Navy SEAL he'd worked with, standing there. The man was now a police officer here in Lantern Beach.

The two shook hands.

"I heard you were on the island." Gunner paused and placed his hands on his hips. "I'm surprised it's taken me this long to run into you."

"Been working a lot lately." Dillinger shrugged. "Plus, I have two kids at home now, and my wife runs a restaurant. Having a family changes everything. But it's great. I love it. I really do."

"I bet. Good for you."

Dillinger's grin faded. "It's a real shame what happened on the island tonight, isn't it?"

Dillinger nodded toward Noelle's room.

Gunner's back muscles tightened at the memories.

"It really is. Noelle is a nice woman. She didn't deserve this."

"I can't help but wonder if this has something to do with Ocean Essence. It's been all the talk of the island since it opened here six months ago."

Gunner had heard various people on the island talking about the lab. "It does seem like an odd location for a lab, doesn't it?"

"It does. This island is the perfect location for a person or organization looking for privacy and seclusion." Dillinger raised his eyebrows, letting his statement hang out there.

Gunner didn't like the thought of that. He'd encountered too many evil men, men intent on destroying anything that got in the way of their quest for power and money.

He supposed he'd become a tad jaded over the years as a SEAL, dealing with the worst of humanity.

"What are you still doing here anyway?" Dillinger shifted the subject and studied Gunner instead.

"I thought maybe you could use a second set of eyes in case this man comes back."

"Not a bad idea, but he'd have to be pretty brazen to come to the clinic. Besides, if he'd wanted to kill Noelle, he could have, right?"

"That's true." Gunner ran a hand over his mouth to hide his frown. "But he obviously wanted something from her. The question is, what?"

Someone called to Dillinger from the lobby, and Dillinger excused himself.

As he did, Gunner paced to the other end of the hallway, toward an emergency exit.

He peered outside through the small window in the door.

A light bobbed in the distance.

Almost like a flashlight bouncing as someone carried it.

There was a patch of woods back there.

Was someone walking through them?

Why would anyone be out there at this time of night?

A bad feeling gurgled inside him.

Then he saw a flash.

Someone was taking pictures of this place, he realized.

His gut tightened.

There was no good reason for someone to be doing that at this time of night.

Unless this had something to do with Noelle.

He reached for the handle to push the door open, but he stopped himself.

If he left right now, he'd be leaving Noelle alone. The best thing he could do was to stay close to her.

But he'd find Dillinger and let the officer know what was going on.

Because the mystery around Noelle Purdy continued to deepen . . . and so did the danger.

CHAPTER
TEN

JUST AS EXPECTED, Noelle was sore the next morning.

Her entire body ached, and she didn't even want to look in the mirror to see what her swollen face looked like.

But those were the least of her concerns.

Mostly, she thought about her mom. About the danger she could be in.

Her thoughts continued to turn over as she tried to put the pieces together.

How had that man gotten into her house last night? How had he slipped past her security system?

Cassidy had stopped by again and brought her cell phone. She'd told Noelle that her officers had checked out her place, and nothing appeared to be missing—that they could tell.

Then Noelle had helped Cassidy check her security footage. There was nothing there.

She knew these men were smart. That they had technology that allowed them to do whatever they wanted.

They must have bypassed her system somehow.

She didn't have enough energy right now to figure out how they did it. But she didn't like the thought of it.

Doc Clemson, a jolly man close to retirement, came into Noelle's room at seven and said she'd be discharged to leave soon. He gave her some pain meds just in case she needed them, but she'd try not to take them. She'd push through on her own if she could.

Then she called Rachel and gave her a brief overview of what had happened. Rachel gasped before promising to be right out to give her a ride.

While Noelle waited, she did her best to fix herself up.

She didn't have a change of clothes here or even makeup. But she pulled her hair back into a loose ponytail and splashed some water on her face.

When she raised her head, she got a glimpse of herself in the mirror.

She was unable to look away—much like watching an accident.

Half her face was swollen. The bruise around one of her eyes was large and dark. Her lip was partially busted, and a small cut ran alongside her ear.

There would be no hiding what had happened to her. As soon as people got one look at Noelle's face, they'd know she'd been through something terrible.

Then she'd need to explain.

Noelle would need to come up with a good story—

one that contained the truth, but not *too much* of the truth. Just enough to get people to stop asking questions. Just enough to keep her mother safe.

A few minutes later, as she sat on the edge of the bed, Rachel rushed into the room. Her dark hair tumbled into her face, and her expressive eyes displayed her worry.

Her gaze widened when she caught a glimpse of Noelle.

"Oh, Noelle . . . I'm so sorry." Rachel paused in front of her, concern showing in the crease between her eyes. "You should've called earlier."

"I was being taken care of, and I didn't want to worry you." Her throat burned as the seriousness of the situation hit her again.

Rachel gingerly lowered herself onto the edge of the bed. "I'm your friend. That's what I'm supposed to do."

Noelle squeezed her friend's hand. "I know. I'm just glad that you're here now."

Rachel stared at her another moment before frowning. Then she seemed to remind herself to stay calm, and her expression cleared into a more leveled one. "What can I do for you?"

"I need to get cleaned up. And I know this might sound crazy, but then I'd like to go to church."

Noelle had already thought it through. The other alternative would be going home with Rachel, which could then mean putting Rachel in danger. Or she could go back to her own house. But she wouldn't feel safe alone there either.

She supposed there were other people at the lab she could call. But she wasn't particularly close to any of them.

Eventually, she'd need a better game plan. But she needed more time first.

"Let's go to my house, and you can borrow some of my clothes and get cleaned up," Rachel offered. "If you really want to go to church, then I say, let's do it." She glanced at her watch. "We have an hour and a half to get there. Is that enough time?"

"I've already signed the discharge papers."

Rachel stood. "Perfect then. Should I get a nurse to wheel you out? That seems to be the protocol when you go home."

Noelle knew the routine. She'd spent two weeks in the hospital after Gunner had rescued her two years ago. She'd been dehydrated and needed a battery of medical tests. That wasn't to mention the litany of questioning she'd gone through with government agents. She wasn't even sure which branch those agents had been with. Military? FBI?

Going over and over everything that had happened had been more exhausting than the medical testing and recovery.

Returning to the present, Noelle forced a light smile. "That would be great."

A few minutes later, when Rachel pushed her into the hallway, Noelle found herself searching for Gunner.

She wasn't sure why. Except that a few times during the night when the door opened, she'd thought she spotted him sitting in the hallway. She'd asked one of the nurses about it, and the nurse had told her he'd insisted on keeping guard. Even though it was past visiting hours, the clinic administration had made an exception.

Noelle wasn't sure how that made her feel. Safe, she supposed.

Something about Gunner seemed to indicate he knew more than the average person did about her. They'd shared a bond forged in tragedy. Even though they didn't really know each other, Noelle somehow felt close to him.

"Let's get you out of here." Rachel nodded toward the door.

Noelle would have to resume normal life again.

She'd done it before. After losing her baby. After her divorce. After her abduction. Her mom's disappearance.

And she could do it again.

However, she knew danger was still close. That the man *would* reappear again. That he'd make demands that she'd be unable to say no to.

But how could Noelle live with herself if she said yes?

She frowned.

She knew the answer to that question.

She couldn't.

———

On the drive to Rachel's house, Noelle gave her friend a recap of what had happened . . . minus the man's demand.

Her friend gasped and shook her head with every new detail.

"That's just unbelievable," Rachel murmured as she gripped the steering wheel.

The roads were more crowded than usual. Tourists were already out, surfboards balanced on their heads and beach wagons loaded with toys being pulled behind them.

But otherwise, the sun cast a low morning glow, making everything appear as if it were bathed in lemonade around her.

"I'm still having trouble believing this isn't just some type of nightmare I need to wake up from." Noelle rubbed her arms as a chill washed over her.

"I'm worried for you." Rachel cast a concerned glance at her.

Noelle wished she could tell her friend about the threat against her mom. That she could tell *someone* about her deepest worries.

But that man said if she did her mom would die.

He had to be connected with the Alphas. Those men were conniving and manipulative, the type to plant listening devices—to do whatever it took to get what they wanted. They'd obviously gotten through her security system already.

Noelle couldn't take any risks.

She glanced at Rachel's house in the distance as they approached it. "Is Jonah going to be at church today?"

A shadow rolled over her friend's gaze. "He had to leave. He had some time off work for a while, but now he has jobs to do if he wants to keep his position at the company. I'm not sure when he'll be back."

Rachel and Jonah seemed like a match made in heaven. But Noelle knew Jonah worked some type of consulting job that required travel. He hadn't intended on settling down here, from what Noelle understood. Lantern Beach wasn't exactly a convenient spot for people who had to fly across the country on a regular basis.

In fact, getting to the airport required taking two ferries and then driving nearly three hours.

But Noelle had felt confident the two of them, if anyone, could make their relationship work.

"You really don't know when he'll be back?" Noelle tried to read between the lines of her friend's statements.

Rachel glanced at her again, but her smile looked forced. "No, not right now. We have some things we need to work out."

Noelle didn't ask any more questions. It was better if she didn't right now.

She liked Jonah, and Rachel had seemed so happy with him.

Noelle hoped things worked out between the two.

"Okay, enough talking." Rachel parked in her driveway and opened her car door with a resigned sigh.

"If we're going to be on time for church, then we need to get you ready."

Noelle couldn't argue with that.

But another part of her dreaded what today might hold.

Would the man return again?

As if right on cue, her phone buzzed.

It was a picture of the Lantern Beach Medical Clinic. Based on the darkness, it had been taken last night.

Then a message followed.

I'm watching you.

CHAPTER
ELEVEN

NOELLE FELT MORE self-conscious than she would have liked as she stepped into church. She and Rachel were three minutes late, so praise and worship had already begun. At least that helped everyone not to turn and stare at her.

Rachel had helped Noelle use makeup to conceal her wounds. The coverup worked pretty well—at first glance.

Upon closer inspection, anyone could see that Noelle had been beaten. It wasn't a pretty sight.

She drew in a shaky breath at the thought. She was the one who had chosen to come here today, and she'd known this was a risk.

But coming to church always made her feel better. Right now, she needed to stop thinking about herself and concentrate on worship.

As she and Rachel slid into a pew in the back, Noelle scanned the small congregation.

Her gaze stopped when she saw Gunner beside Ty and Cassidy. He was dressed in khakis and a white polo with sleeves that hugged his biceps.

He looked rugged yet distinguished.

Definitely handsome. Very handsome.

He seemed to sense her watching him and glanced over his shoulder. His eyes widened with surprise when he saw her, and he offered a small wave.

Noelle waved back.

The same rush of attraction swept over her again, and she chided herself.

No hero complexes allowed.

Instead, she concentrated on the lyrics on the screen at the front of the church as they sang "Way Maker."

Only halfway through the song, someone appeared beside her.

Her entire body tensed.

When she looked up, she saw her new friend Rex Houghton.

Relief swept through her.

She'd halfway been expecting to see her attacker standing there.

She nearly laughed at herself. After all, what kind of criminal would show up in church to harm her?

Then again, the world had gone crazy these days.

"May I sit here?" he whispered.

She nodded and scooted down farther to make room for him.

She'd met Rex at a restaurant a few weeks ago, and the two of them had been talking since then.

They'd even gone out to eat together a couple of times.

The man seemed nice enough. And he seemed interested in her—as more than friends.

But Noelle wasn't interested in dating, even if the man was attractive.

But she was hesitant to get involved in any relationship. Especially after Josh.

She'd thought Josh had been so perfect. But when the going had gotten tough, he'd left her.

It was part of the reason she'd taken that job in France. So she could start fresh.

That had turned out to be a bad idea also.

Three months after she arrived, her mom's health had begun to go downhill. Noelle had been in the midst of making some choices about the future and whether or not she should move back to the States.

She hadn't had a chance to decide—because she'd been abducted.

Afterward, moving back to the States and starting fresh had been a no brainer. Noelle had placed her mother in a memory care facility an hour and a half away and had gone to see her every weekend—even if her mom no longer remembered her.

Sadness pressed on her.

Again, Noelle turned her thoughts away from Rex and Gunner and Josh and her mom—and every other distraction—and tried to concentrate on worshipping.

Just as the singing ended and they sat down to listen to the sermon, her phone buzzed.

Noelle usually didn't answer during church.

But for some reason, she glanced at her screen.

She'd gotten another text.

She should have ignored it.

The words there caused her blood to go cold.

> If you want your mom to live, pay attention.

Gunner struggled through church.

Coming here with Ty and Cassidy today was one of the requirements they'd given him if he wanted to stay past the end of the Hope House session.

And he did want to stay longer.

That was the only reason he was here at Lantern Beach Community Church today.

He hadn't stepped foot in a church since his accident. He'd told himself he never would. Coming here was just a matter of going through the motions, and nothing more.

Then he'd seen Noelle come in.

His heart had begun to race. He'd stayed at the hospital until six a.m. when Dillinger's shift had ended and another officer had taken his place. Then Gunner had caught a ride with Dillinger back to Hope House.

He'd been trying to think of excuses to see Noelle again today.

Now here she was.

Then Rex Houghton had changed seats so he could sit beside her.

A growl formed in his chest at the thought.

Gunner had met the guy last week while he and Ty were out jogging.

The man was in his thirties with a ruddy complexion and thick light-brown hair. Something about the way he dressed and carried himself made it clear he had money and thought of himself as highly intelligent.

He owned some type of company and had moved here to start a think tank.

Who did that?

Why did the thought of Noelle sitting beside that man bring Gunner a surge of discomfort? Maybe even jealousy?

The reaction made no sense.

But if Gunner were honest with himself, that was how he felt.

The words of the sermon drifted to his ears—a sermon on forgiveness—forgiving others as well as yourself. It was almost as if Pastor Jack had written it just for Gunner.

But he was a long way from forgiving himself. In fact, the action didn't even seem like a possibility. Men had died under his watch. That was something he'd never move past. If someone he knew had been a mole, then he should have known. Should have been able to sniff him out.

Finally, the service ended.

Gunner couldn't wait to get out of here.

But Ty and Cassidy were his ride, so their departure probably wouldn't be quick. They seemed to have a lot of friends in the church and introduced him to several of them.

Gunner tried to pay attention to names and faces, but his gaze kept wandering across the room to Noelle.

He frowned when he saw her still talking to Rex. The man—charming in his own eyes, no doubt—said something that made her laugh.

It was a beautiful sight to see her throw her head back. To see a smile on her face.

Something uncommon in the time he'd been around her.

But something he'd love to see more.

His phone buzzed, jerking his attention away.

He'd put in a call last night to one of his former colleagues, a CIA agent he'd worked with on several occasions. Now Pete Honeycutt was calling back.

Gunner slipped away to answer, figuring it was a good excuse to avoid the discomfort caused by being in church and seeing Rex set his sights on Noelle.

He placed the phone to his ear as he stepped outside. "Hey, Pete. Thanks for calling me back."

"No problem." Pete's Southern drawl stretched over the line—a drawl that could disappear at a moment's notice if Pete needed to transform into someone else and go undercover. "I figure you have a good reason for asking about the Alphas."

"I do. But I'd rather not share that reason for the time being." Gunner glanced around, searching for anyone suspicious or that might be close enough to listen in.

He saw no one.

"No problem," his friend said. "I don't know a lot about them. But here's what I can tell you. They're flashy. They're manipulative. They like to play games."

Gunner agreed with those observations. He'd always thought the ransom demand was just a front to distract them from what the group was really doing.

"We thought they disbanded," Pete continued. "But the truth is, there are a lot of rumors that they not only didn't disband, but they've grown in numbers and are stronger than ever."

"That's not what I wanted to hear." Gunner's back muscles tightened so quickly they nearly ached. "Sounds like they're planning something."

"They are planning something. I don't know what, but I know that some of my contacts within the CIA are keeping a close eye on them."

Was someone from the Alphas still terrorizing Noelle? Were they upset because she'd gotten away?

Gunner didn't know.

But he did remember raiding their compound.

Before he'd rescued Noelle, he and two of his guys had stumbled upon a lab set up near her room.

He couldn't help but wonder if that lab was the reason those men had abducted Noelle in the first place. Yet she'd never mentioned it.

As far as everyone knew, she and her colleagues had been abducted for financial reasons.

But that had never made sense to Gunner.

And his two colleagues—the ones who'd seen the lab along with him—had been killed in the explosion.

Then the compound had been blown up, destroying any proof the lab ever existed.

Gunner's commander never seemed to think much of it. He'd muttered that the place used to be a hospital.

But Gunner had always wondered if there was more to that story.

Was that the reason the Alphas might be back also?

Did whatever they were planning have to do with Noelle?

He didn't know.

But the possibility wouldn't leave his mind.

NOELLE WATCHED Gunner put the phone to his ear as he left the sanctuary. What was that about? Why did he look so serious?

Whatever he was doing, it was none of her business. But she was curious about the man. Curious about whether he was still a SEAL. Curious about what he was doing here. About what his life looked like now.

"So what do you say?"

Noelle glanced up and realized that Rex had been talking to her.

She'd totally tuned him out. He'd already asked her about her wounds, and she'd mumbled some excuse about falling.

She technically *had* fallen . . . if being shoved to the ground was the same thing as stumbling.

Noelle frowned. She didn't like deceiving people. But she didn't want everyone to know her business either.

"I'm sorry, but what was that again?"

A slightly annoyed expression flickered across Rex's gaze before quickly disappearing. No doubt he was used to people hanging onto his every word.

"I said I want to go to dinner with you again sometime." Rex's eyes sparkled with hope and confidence. "What do you think?"

What *did* she think about that? Noelle had no reason not to go. Dating was how people got to know each other, right? It wasn't as if Noelle was promising to marry this guy.

Though part of her didn't want to date anyone again after Josh, Rachel had encouraged her to put herself out there again. She'd said that otherwise, Josh would win.

Noelle couldn't let him do that.

"I think that would be nice. But maybe not this week." Noelle pointed at her face. "I have some follow-up appointments I need to schedule, so I don't know what my calendar is going to be like."

Rex nodded, understanding in his gaze. "Of course. Whenever you're ready."

Someone across the sanctuary called to him, and he excused himself.

As he wandered away, Cassidy and Ty approached her.

"Good to see you here this morning." Ty flashed a friendly grin.

She'd always admired the man. He was kind and tough, an unusual combination. But his sacrificial spirit and willingness to help others was clear.

Noelle returned his smile. "Good to be here."

Cassidy studied Noelle's face a moment before asking, "How are you doing today?"

Noelle shrugged. "I've been better. But I'm grateful to be alive."

She *was* grateful to be alive. However, she couldn't ignore the feeling that an impending storm was heading her way and that being alive might soon be a thing of the past.

"We're grateful you're alive too." Cassidy lowered her voice as she stepped closer. "I want you to know that we're doing everything we can to find the person who did this to you."

"I appreciate that." The sincerity in the chief's voice caused a surge of gratitude to fill her.

Noelle really was fortunate to be in a place where people cared, where she wasn't brushed off or seen as just another face in the crowd. Now that she'd experienced small-town living, she wasn't sure she could ever go back to the city.

Cassidy shifted, her striped blue-and-white sundress and white sweater making her seem more like an average, everyday woman than a superhero police chief—at least that was how she came across in Noelle's mind.

"Listen, Ty and I are having some people over for lunch today," Cassidy started. "We're going to throw some meat on the grill, play volleyball, and try to take it easy. Would you like to come? Bring Rachel too. And Jonah if he's in town."

"We'd love to." Rachel popped into the conversation. She grabbed Noelle's arm and grinned. "That sounds fun, doesn't it?"

Noelle reluctantly nodded. Part of her wanted to seclude herself today. To stay away from people. To decompress.

But being alone also sounded . . . frightening.

She forced a smile. "Sure. But I'm sure it would be against doctor's orders for me to play volleyball."

"Then just come and hang out," Cassidy said. "We'd love to have you."

"That sounds great."

As soon as Cassidy walked away, Rachel leaned closer. "Sorry for jumping in. I had a feeling you were going to say no."

"I was."

"I think it will be good for you to get out."

Noelle raised her eyebrows as she turned toward Rachel and gave her a look.

Rachel shrugged. "What? I'm just trying to look out for you. And that brooding, mysteriously handsome guy with Ty and Cassidy could be the perfect distraction for you."

"Gunner?" Noelle practically spit out his name. She knew she was acting as if the thought was absurd—though it was anything but.

She couldn't let anyone know how she really felt, though. Not given the fact that Gunner clearly didn't like her.

But now they were going to the cookout. That most

likely meant Noelle would be around Gunner again—just as Rachel had hoped.

She hid her frown before anyone could see it. Hanging out with the man wasn't at the top of her list.

If there was anyone who could see through her and figure out what was really going on inside her head, it would be Gunner.

Therefore, Noelle needed to be very careful how she proceeded.

As she stood there, she glanced around.

Why did she suddenly feel as if she were being watched?

She saw no one suspicious.

But could the guy who'd beaten her be working with someone else? And could that person be here?

She hadn't been in Lantern Beach long enough to recognize all the locals. That wasn't to mention the flux of visitors they had right now.

She remembered the dirt room where she'd been kept during her abduction.

She couldn't go back to a place like that.

She just couldn't.

———

Gunner tried to relax as he helped Ty grill the meat.

Almost twenty people had shown up, including Ty's parents and Braden Dillinger and his wife, Lisa. Other people from their Bible study group were here as well as a few people who worked for Blackout, the private security firm that Ty had started.

Gunner recognized several faces—Colton Locke and his wife, Elise. Brandon Hale and his fiancée, Finley. Axel Hendrix and his fiancée, Olivia.

When the chicken and steaks were done, everyone grabbed a plate of food and went to the beach to enjoy themselves.

Since Noelle had arrived here for the cookout, she and Gunner had yet to talk.

Instead, Noelle had mostly chatted with Rachel and Cassidy.

They'd both seemed to purposefully keep themselves occupied doing other things.

Every time Gunner glanced at her, he tried not to stare at the bruises on her face. Though Noelle had attempted to cover them up, they still peeked through her makeup like ghosts of the past. Every time he caught a glimpse of her injuries, a new surge of anger rose in him.

Someone thought they would get away with doing that to her. But Gunner would make sure this person was found.

In fact, part of Gunner didn't even want to stay at the cookout. He wanted to hit the streets and find the person responsible.

But he knew that would be an exercise in futility.

He had no idea where to look and wandering aimlessly around the island would do no one any good. At least right now, he was with Noelle and could keep a lookout for trouble. He just had to make sure he didn't hover too close or overstep.

After eating, Ty gathered everyone for a game of volleyball.

Noelle held Faith as everyone else either played or cleaned up. It would have been a bad idea for her to try to join considering her injuries.

Maybe it was a bad idea for him to play with his leg.

But he was going to try anyway.

He used to love the game. This would be the first time he'd played since the accident. However, he wore joggers, not quite ready for everyone to see his prosthetic.

But he felt something stirring inside him. Something he hadn't felt in a long time.

A desire to join in.

He wasn't sure why it was happening now. But he wasn't complaining.

It felt good to branch outside his comfort zone. It had been a long time.

They were in the middle of their first set when Cassidy's phone rang. As she left the game, the ball hit the sand, scoring his team another point.

His teammates let out a whoop as they won their set.

He wished he could feel victorious. But he sensed something was going on.

He tried not to listen to the snippets of conversation that drifted through the breeze as everyone took a quick water break. But based on Cassidy's uptight body motions, he had a feeling whoever was on the other line wasn't sharing good news.

When Cassidy ended the call, she motioned to Ty.

Ty grabbed the ball and placed it against his hip as he turned to her. "Everything okay?"

Gunner was still close enough to hear their conversation—and he couldn't seem to stop himself from listening. Not considering everything that had happened. He was eager for answers, for resolution.

"That was Bradshaw," Cassidy said. "Someone reported some strange activity at a local cemetery, so he went by. Three graves have been dug up."

Gunner raised his eyebrows. Someone was digging up graves?

What in the world . . . ?

He glanced at Noelle and saw she'd gone deathly pale. Something about Cassidy's words had triggered something in her. A memory maybe?

Though he didn't remember anything about graves from his rescue mission, he was certain there had been a lab set up. Given Noelle's scientific expertise, could all of this be linked?

His gut told him yes.

But if that was true . . . why wasn't Noelle admitting it? Why keep secrets?

Unless she was somehow involved?

What if they Alphas had convinced her to be a part of their team?

Was that thought extreme?

Maybe.

But he'd seen crazier things happen.

And there was something about Noelle's story that had never made sense to him. She said she was in the dirty cell for her abduction. Yet she looked clean. Well fed. She'd smelled faintly of chemicals.

She knew more about these crimes than she was letting on, didn't she? Did she know who the mole was who'd gotten two of his team members killed?

His gut tightened.

Trouble was on this island.

Trouble connected with his last mission as a SEAL.

Possibly trouble that had caused him to lose his leg.

Trouble that may have led to Noelle's abduction.

He had a feeling the Alphas were on the island. That they were the ones behind everything. These tactics . . . they fit the group.

But what exactly was the group planning now?

CHAPTER
THIRTEEN

NOELLE'S HEART RACED.

Disturbed graves?

A chill washed through her until her head spun. Why did that sound familiar?

Nothing made sense right now.

She took a few steps back toward the sand dune and, holding Faith carefully, she sat down before she passed out.

The last thing she wanted was to draw attention to herself. Sitting down seemed a better option than falling over with Faith in her arms.

"Do we need to get you back to the clinic?" Cassidy walked closer and took Faith, handing the toddler to her friend Skye instead.

Noelle shook her head, unsure what she could say. But it would be hard to gloss this over and pretend like her reaction was nothing.

"I'm fine," she finally croaked. "Just lightheaded from yesterday's injuries, I guess."

"I need to leave and investigate something with Bradshaw." Cassidy's eyes narrowed as she observed Noelle. "Is there anything you need to tell me?"

"Wait . . ." Rachel joined their circle. "You don't think Noelle dug up the graves, do you?"

"Of course not," Cassidy said. "But I know something strange is happening. I believe these incidents that have occurred recently on the island could be linked."

Gunner stepped closer. "Tell her, Noelle. Whatever it is you know, you need to stop holding it inside."

Noelle's heart pounded harder as her gaze jerked up to meet his.

How dare he come over here and say something like that? Attention was not what she wanted right now.

She glanced to the crowd around them.

Several people averted their gazes and stepped away.

"Someone needs to start talking." Cassidy crossed her arms as she looked from Noelle to Gunner and back again. "I don't like being kept in the dark."

Noelle drew in a deep breath, trying to calm her racing thoughts. But she couldn't ignore the surge of anger she felt.

She didn't want to be in this position. And she *definitely* didn't want an audience.

Did Gunner know what that man had told her? That he had her mother?

If so . . . how? How would he know that?

"Not here." She stood and brushed the sand from her legs and arms.

"Let's go inside." Cassidy nodded toward the house.

Cassidy, Noelle, and Gunner filed inside. Once there, they stood stiffly in a semi-circle, and Cassidy waited.

Noelle drew in several deep breaths before turning to Gunner. "What exactly are you accusing me of?"

"You know more than you're letting on."

"What are you talking about?"

His gaze darkened. "When I rescued you, I saw a lab in the facility. I have no proof it was there because the whole building exploded, leaving no evidence behind."

"Why would there be a lab in the building?" Her voice climbed with tension.

"You tell me." He stared at her, waiting for her response.

Her thoughts raced again. She remembered that test tube that had flashed into her thoughts. The equipment. The other images that she kept having flashbacks about.

But she had no real memories of them.

Were those objects somehow connected with her mother's abduction?

Was all of this related?

"Noelle . . ." Cassidy stared at her. "What are you thinking? Do you know something that you're keeping from us?"

She swallowed hard. How could she share something so vague?

This might not be anything.

"Are you secretly working for Russia?" Gunner demanded, a hard look in his eyes.

"Like, as a spy?" Her voice rose with shock. "No. How could you even ask that?"

"Something isn't adding up, Noelle. And you're the only one who can tell us what."

She glared at him, not appreciating the insinuations. "I told everyone what happened. It was a ransom demand and nothing else."

"Then why did you look shaken up when she mentioned some graves being disturbed?"

"I . . . I don't know." That was an excellent question.

Cassidy narrowed her gaze. "I don't know what's going on here, but I told you before I don't like being left in the dark."

Noelle swallowed hard. "I'm not trying to keep you in the dark. I promise."

"I'd like you to come with me to the cemetery." A new resolve filled Cassidy's voice.

"Why?" Noelle's voice tightened. "How's that going to help?"

"I'm not sure. I just know I want you there."

"Of course," Noelle murmured, figuring she had nothing to hide. "Whatever I can do."

"I'd like to go also." Gunner stepped forward.

Cassidy hesitated a moment as if contemplating her response. Finally, she nodded. "Okay. But you need to drive separately."

"I'll ride with him," Noelle said before adding, "if that's okay."

She wasn't sure where the words had come from. But riding together might be a good opportunity for the two of them to talk alone.

Why did he suspect her of being a spy?

What exactly did he see before her rescue? Did he know something that she didn't?

Was there more to that story than she ever realized?

Wasn't that what her subconscious seemed to be hinting at anyway?

———

Gunner opened the door for Noelle and waited for her to climb inside his cobalt blue Jeep Wrangler.

His mom had raised him with some manners, and there were some things a guy never forgot. Helping a woman into his vehicle was one of them—even if she might be a spy.

His spine tightened at the thought.

Then he climbed inside and waited until Cassidy had pulled away before he followed down the road behind her.

The island wasn't that big, so he and Noelle didn't have much time to talk. But he had a lot of questions.

"Is there anything you need to tell me before we get there?" Gunner cast a quick glance at Noelle.

Noelle still looked painfully pale as she gazed out

the window. Her motions were stiff and nearly lethargic —which worried him.

"I don't appreciate your insinuations." She crossed her arms and stared out the window.

"You and I both know there was more to your abduction than you're letting on."

"No, there wasn't."

"So it was just a coincidence that lab was there?" He needed to know the truth.

"I don't remember a lab!"

He cast her a skeptical glance.

"I don't," she reiterated. "Was it old? From when the place used to be a hospital?"

"No, everything appeared new and state of the art. It can't be a coincidence that they abducted three scientists *and* had that lab there."

"No one has ever mentioned it to me before. It didn't come up when I was debriefed."

"I'm the only one who saw it. My two colleagues . . ." He swallowed hard. "They were killed, as you might have heard."

She cast him a quick, apologetic glance. "I'm sorry."

"But there's more to the story. I'm certain of it."

"I don't know what to tell you. It's been two years since you rescued me." Her voice sounded strained as she started. "And I've tried to put my kidnapping behind me and move on. Life has pretty much returned to normal. But now, for some reason, whatever happened to me in Russia seems to be coming back to the surface. I have no idea why. Is it because you're on the island?"

Gunner flinched at her words. "Why would I have anything to do with this?"

"I'm just saying the timing is strange."

So she was turning the tables and looking at him now?

Clever.

"These guys haven't come after me," he reminded her. "They don't even know who I am, as far as I know. Are you saying you have no idea why they could be coming after you now?"

Noelle opened her mouth then shut it again.

Gunner knew that there was more to this.

Fear was keeping her quiet about something, wasn't it?

"You can talk to me." His voice sounded gravelly as he said the words.

He needed her to trust him. But he'd done a poor job cultivating that trust over the past couple of days. Other than helping her on the beach, he hadn't exactly been friendly toward her.

"I've . . ." Noelle opened her mouth but shut it again. Then she leaned forward and rubbed her temples, her breathing too shallow for comfort. "I feel like I could pass out."

Gunner put a hand on her shoulder and nudged her until she was sitting upright. "Open up your diaphragm. Take a deep breath. Hold it. Release it."

Noelle did as he instructed.

Before he could ask her any more questions, Cassidy braked and pulled off onto a side road.

Gunner drove in beside her as she parked next to two other police cruisers already at the scene.

As his Jeep came to a stop, Gunner glanced out the windshield at the tombstones in front of him, tombstones that were surrounded by a patch of trees and several beach homes on the sound side of the island.

He'd expected a cemetery to be located near a church or something. Not near beach houses.

However, the cemetery looked old. Really old.

Gunner wanted more answers from Noelle.

But his questions would have to wait.

It was time to face this grisly scene.

He only hoped Noelle was up for this.

CASSIDY DIDN'T KNOW what was going on. But somehow, these crimes were linked to both Noelle's and Gunner's pasts. She felt certain of it.

Had God aligned things to bring the two of them to the island at the same time?

After all, Noelle had been on the island since late fall, and Gunner had applied to be a part of Hope House back in December.

Neither of the two knew that each other would be here. They hadn't planned it together. The idea that someone had been keeping an eye on both of them and waiting for just the moment when they might be together again seemed too far-fetched.

Had someone somehow orchestrated this?

Cassidy wasn't sure about the details from Noelle's abduction and when Gunner had saved her. But she had a feeling that whatever trouble had happened two years ago had shown up here on Lantern Beach now.

Why would those men who'd abducted Noelle have exhumed dead bodies? Why had they taken Noelle?

She wasn't sure, but she didn't like the thought of these men digging around her town and stirring up trouble.

And why would those men find Noelle now?

What had changed to propel them into action after being dormant for two years?

Or maybe they had been active somewhere else.

Cassidy's stomach twisted into a knot at the thought.

She would save the rest of her questions for Noelle until later.

For now, Cassidy climbed out of her SUV and walked toward the small cemetery. Some of the graves went back at least a hundred fifty years. Several cemetery plots like this were located on the island, back from the days of the early settlers.

As development had occurred on Lantern Beach, homes had popped up all around the family cemeteries. But the graves remained where they were, the remains of the dead undisturbed.

Until today.

Cassidy approached Officer Bradshaw, her point of contact.

"Another exciting day here on Lantern Beach," she muttered as her gaze went to three graves.

Fresh piles of sandy grass had been placed in mounds beside the weathered tombstones.

The coffins, once buried in the ground, had been opened and were now empty.

"This is a Class H felony in North Carolina," Bradshaw murmured. "Exciting for sure."

"Any signs of the bodies?" Cassidy asked Bradshaw.

Officer Bradshaw stood at the edge of the hole, his hands on his hips and sunglasses across his eyes. "None."

She stared at the coffins. "They look pretty standard, not something that someone wealthy would have. I can only assume there were no valuables inside."

"That's my impression also," Bradshaw said.

"No one saw anything?"

"No one that I've talked to."

"How old are these burials?" Cassidy asked.

"They were all from around 1949."

Cassidy glanced at Noelle, who stood silently beside a small fence made out of ornamental concrete blocks. Her skin looked pale and her gaze shell-shocked as she stared at the scene.

"Any thoughts on this?" Cassidy asked.

Noelle dragged her eyes from the scene and met Cassidy's gaze. "I . . . I don't know. It could be a coincidence."

"What could be a coincidence?"

She pressed her lips together. "I'm hesitant to even state my theory aloud."

"Why?"

"Because, if I'm right, then we're all in trouble."

NOELLE FELT as if she might pass out.

Gunner seemed to sense that and touched her elbow. "Maybe you should sit down."

She'd never had a proclivity for fainting before. She wasn't sure why she felt the urge so strongly today—twice now. Maybe she'd blame it on her head injury or the surprisingly warm weather as the sun beat down on them.

But she knew neither of those things were the reason why.

"Let's go to my car so you can sit down," Cassidy muttered.

Gunner led Noelle to the SUV. Cassidy opened the passenger door, and Noelle climbed inside, sagging against the seat while Gunner and Cassidy remained outside with the door open.

"So?" Cassidy glanced back and forth between the two of them as if waiting for someone to explain.

Noelle didn't know how much she could say. Her mom's image flashed into her mind, and reality hit her, reminding her of the stakes.

She had to protect her mom, whatever the cost.

As another thought hit her, she glanced around.

What if an Alpha was watching her right now?

When she glanced at one of the beach houses in the distance, she saw a curtain move.

Could those men be in that house watching? Or had that just been a rubbernecker trying to figure out what was going on with the police cars outside?

"Noelle?" Cassidy stared at her.

She turned her gaze back to Cassidy, and a shiver raked through her.

Noelle didn't like being indecisive. But right now, she had no idea how to handle the situation.

If she messed up, her mom would be killed.

Maybe there was even more to it than that.

Noelle licked her lips and lifted up a quick prayer.

"When I heard the dates of those graves that had been uncovered, it triggered a memory," she started.

Cassidy narrowed her gaze. "What kind of memory?"

"There was a case several years ago . . . where a terrorist group tried to exhume some bodies in Siberia." She licked her lips, her throat suddenly dry.

"Why?" Gunner asked.

"Because these people had been buried in the permafrost, and their bodies—every part of them—

were basically preserved." Her throat tightened with every new sentence.

"What are you getting at, Noelle?" Cassidy stared at her, her gaze intense and unyielding.

"I'm saying that some people believe that certain viruses have only been eradicated from the surface of the planet. They believe if they dig deep enough, anything can be found." She paused. "The terrorists wanted these bodies because those people had died of . . . smallpox." Her voice cracked. "They hoped the virus had been preserved in the corpses."

"What?" Cassidy's voice climbed higher, but she quickly composed herself. She glanced around before lowering her voice. "So you're telling me that someone could have dug up these graves because they're trying to resurrect an extinct disease as a matter of biological warfare?"

"I don't know that for sure." Noelle rubbed her arms, still feeling chilled—even though it was nearly eighty degrees and humid outside today. "I only know that it's a distinct possibility. It's the only reason I can think of that terrorists would dig up bodies—if the Alphas are the ones behind this. I don't get the impression this was done by grave robbers. Do you?"

"No, I don't. What did the date have to do with your theory?" Cassidy asked. "You looked as if you had some type of realization when you heard the year."

"The last cases before smallpox was eradicated in this country were in 1949—the same date on those graves. It just seems like too much of a coincidence."

No one said anything a moment as the horror of her statement settled over them.

Then the images hit her again.

The test tubes.

The lab equipment.

Then . . . a gunshot.

Her heart pounded harder.

What did a gunshot have to do with all of that?

"The temperatures here on the island aren't right for that kind of preservation, correct?" Cassidy asked.

"It shouldn't be," Noelle murmured. "I don't know what's going on."

Noelle's phone buzzed, and she jumped.

She glanced at it quickly.

What she saw made her world spin again.

It was a picture of her mom standing by a window looking outside.

The photo was a reminder that one wrong move could change everything . . . and destroy Noelle's entire world.

She couldn't risk that.

But could she risk the lives of innocent Americans instead?

She already knew the answer to that question.

———

For the first time in months, Gunner forgot about his own problems.

Right now, he needed to figure out what was going through Noelle's mind.

Whatever message she'd just gotten had clearly shaken her up.

"What message did you just get on your phone?" Cassidy asked.

"It's just . . . a prescription that's ready at the pharmacy. Pain meds." Noelle pointed to her face.

Gunner knew there was more to it than that. So did Cassidy.

"I need to see your phone, Noelle." Cassidy held out her hand.

"It's nothing." Noelle continued to tense with every second that passed.

"Then prove it by showing me your screen." Cassidy's voice contained a no-nonsense tone.

Tears pushed from her eyes. "I can't."

"Why not?"

Moisture trickled down her cheeks. "They said they'd kill her."

"Kill who?" Gunner demanded.

Finally, Noelle resigned herself and handed her phone over.

"My mom." Her voice cracked.

"Why is someone sending you her picture?" Cassidy asked.

"To let me know they're watching her, and if I mess up, they're going to kill her."

"Kill her?"

Noelle nodded, her eyes glazed with worry. "I'm not

supposed to tell you any of this. I may have just handed my mother her death sentence."

"Death sentence?" Cassidy repeated.

"I can only imagine what they might do to my mom in order to get what they want," Noelle said.

"You said, 'mess up'?" Cassidy continued.

"They want something from me. I'm not sure what. That's the truth."

"I'm glad you told us." Cassidy shifted as she continued to study the photo. "Tell me about your mom."

"She has dementia. She doesn't even remember me. She hasn't for years. When I got back to the States after my abduction, I had to put her into a memory care facility. I couldn't handle taking care of her on my own—not until I knew I was steadier on my feet."

"Makes sense," Cassidy muttered.

"About a month ago, she somehow wandered away from the facility. Local authorities put out a Silver Alert for her. But she was never found. I just assumed she'd probably wandered into the woods and . . . well, died. But no one ever found the body." She sucked in a shaky breath.

"Someone actually took her?" Cassidy confirmed.

"I didn't think so at first. Not until that man broke into my house last night and showed me her photo."

"So there *was* more to that story?" Cassidy didn't try to hide the fact she was studying Noelle for any sign of deception.

"If I said anything, they said they'd kill her. I didn't

know what the stakes were. I didn't know what they were thinking."

"They may be thinking about killing more people than your mother."

She rubbed her temples. "I don't understand all of this."

"It's time we do some digging."

"If they know I told you . . ." Noelle swallowed hard.

"We'll keep it under wraps." Cassidy shifted. "But tell me more about smallpox and dead bodies."

Noelle licked her lips. "If the right person could extract DNA from a pustule of someone who had smallpox, then there's a chance they could find strains of the virus."

"But the virus was eradicated, right?" Gunner confirmed.

"That's correct. But someone with nefarious intentions . . . with the right skills, they could piece the virus together from existing sequences in human DNA. Then they could insert that into a host genome and—" She frowned. "I won't get too scientific. But there's a possibility of a pandemic."

No one said anything a moment.

Finally, Noelle cleared her throat. "I'm sure you probably know this, but up to thirty percent of the people infected with smallpox died. Millions of people."

"Are you sure that's what this is about?" Gunner narrowed his eyes as he studied her face.

"No, not at all. But when you put the pieces together, it makes sense."

"It does," Cassidy agreed. "The question is . . . what do you have that they want, Noelle?"

Noelle went pale again—deathly pale. "Knowledge. Skills. Education. But you have to know that I would never use my knowledge for anything like that."

Cassidy stared at her another moment.

"I think she needs to go home and lie down," Gunner said.

Noelle glanced at him, a flutter of gratitude in her eyes.

But Cassidy's gaze remained hard. She wasn't going to let this drop.

But maybe she'd give them a break . . . for now, at least.

Gunner waited for her decision.

Finally, the police chief nodded. "Fine. Would you mind driving her back to her house and staying with her? But we *will* need to talk later."

Cassidy gave her a pointed look.

Noelle nodded. "Of course."

"And Noelle . . . if you're right, this is bigger than what I can handle," Cassidy said. "I'm going to have to call in the feds. The CDC. Probably other agencies as well."

"That's a good idea." Noelle sounded resigned as she made the statement. "But right now, we have no proof. Just this crazy idea."

"You're right. We'll need more evidence first."

Noelle was putting everything on the line by telling them this. Her mom's life. Her career.

Everything important to her was in jeopardy.

"I'll keep this theory quiet for now," Cassidy said. "But if I wait too long . . . my silence could be detrimental . . . to everyone. I can't let that happen."

With those words, she walked away.

Gunner offered his hand and helped Noelle down from the SUV. He then escorted her to his Jeep.

The truth was, Gunner wasn't ready to let this subject drop. If Noelle knew something that could ultimately protect innocent people, then she needed to share.

But how would Gunner convince her of that?

CHAPTER
SIXTEEN

NOELLE FELT anxiety swirling inside her as she and Gunner headed down the road.

How long could she hide the rest of the story? The flashbacks she kept having—the ones that made her feel as if she were losing her mind?

Acting hadn't exactly been on her résumé. But that was exactly the survival skill she needed now.

She wished she could explain, could put into words why she instinctually knew she needed to be careful. But she couldn't.

Had something happened to her in Russia that she'd repressed? Some type of memory that had never emerged?

She nibbled on her bottom lip.

She wasn't sure.

But when it came to acting, she'd always been such a terrible liar. She considered it a gift. She generally wasn't prone to not tell the truth because it was so obvious when she did.

Her cheeks turned crimson and sweat popped out on her forehead. Not exactly things she could hide.

But now circumstances were different, and she didn't know what to do.

Thankfully, Gunner didn't say much during the drive. He left her alone with her thoughts.

After she called out directions to her house and they pulled into the driveway, Gunner put his Jeep into Park and took in their surroundings, as if searching for anything that seemed off.

She followed his gaze but saw nothing.

However, he made no effort to get out.

Noelle knew what that meant. He wanted to talk.

Apprehension churned inside her.

Was she ready for this? The longer she spent with Gunner, the less she liked the idea of holding anything back from him.

He turned toward her, his eyes stormy. "What aren't you saying?"

"What makes you think that there's something I'm not say—" Her words came out fast—too fast.

"Noelle . . . I know how the Alphas operate." He shifted, his tight jaw making it clear he was upset. "Why don't you just tell me whatever it is you're keeping to yourself? I'm not going to judge you."

He said that now but . . .

"I . . ." She glanced down at her fingers as she

twisted them in her lap. "I don't like to talk about my time in captivity."

"I don't exactly like to talk about the period of my life surrounding your rescue either." He tapped his leg.

Emotion clogged her throat.

Noelle noticed the way he favored one leg over the other. How he sometimes limped.

At first, she thought maybe he'd hurt his knee.

But as he'd been playing volleyball, part of his pant leg had risen.

She'd seen the prosthetic beneath his joggers.

That's when everything made sense—the change in him, the light that seemed to have faded from him, the struggle in his gaze.

He was having to learn to navigate life without a limb.

"How did that happen?" she asked quietly.

He shrugged quickly. "It's a long story."

"I have time."

"It's not important," he insisted.

"I'd say it's very important."

Gunner let out a breath and scowled.

Noelle was certain he wouldn't answer.

But to her surprise, he did.

"It was after one of my most important missions," he started. "We were ambushed. Two of my guys lost their lives. I guess I'm the lucky one."

Noelle's thoughts shifted as the truth washed over her. "You said it was an important mission."

"It was."

She tried to swallow but hardly could. She had too many thoughts colliding in her head.

"Gunner . . . did that happen after you put me in the helicopter during the rescue?" Panic swelled inside her as the truth tried to form a more complete picture in her mind. "The guys said another copter was coming for you. But as we flew away, I saw the explosion and—"

"Don't worry about it."

She leaned closer as she studied his face, determined to get to the truth. "That's what happened to your leg, wasn't it?"

"Like I said, it's not important." He sounded stiff, like talking about it brought back the pain.

"I beg to differ. You lost your leg rescuing me." How could she not have known that? It seemed as if someone would have told her.

Her thoughts reeled.

Gunner said nothing.

But she knew the truth.

So Noelle waited.

"The Alphas were waiting for me and my team." His voice sounded hoarse as he finally said the words. "I'm just thankful we got you out in time. But it almost seemed as if they knew we were coming."

Noelle wasn't sure what she was thinking, but she reached over and squeezed his arm. "I'm so sorry, Gunner."

"It's a hazard of the job." He gently pulled out of her grasp.

Noelle got the message. Gunner didn't want her to touch him. She could respect that.

She'd have to remind herself to keep her distance. More than one person had described her as touchy-feely before. Not everyone appreciated that quality.

"It just isn't right," she finally muttered, her gaze fluttering to her house. "It isn't right."

"Sometimes life gives us a bad hand," Gunner said. "And there's nothing we can do but accept our circumstances and make the best of them. That's what Ty says, at least."

That may be true. But things were so much more complicated for Noelle. So much more.

Suddenly, the Jeep felt stuffy. She felt too close to Gunner. Like she couldn't breathe.

"Listen, how about we go inside and talk?" Noelle finally offered. "I could use some water and some cool air. It's been a long weekend, and I think everything that happened is catching up with me."

Gunner's simmering gaze remained on her a few moments before he nodded. "Okay. But I'd like to check the place out before you go inside."

"Of course."

They walked up the stairs to her front door.

But when she got there, she paused.

A picture had been taped on the storm door.

A picture of someone whose skin was filled with blisters. Whose eyes were lit with agony. Whose mouth was open and twisted in a silent scream.

Noelle's head spun until she thought she might throw up.

————

"What is this?" Gunner stared at the photo, hoping his assumptions were wrong.

"It's . . ." Noelle's hand flew over her mouth. "I'm not sure, but I believe it's someone with . . . smallpox."

Realization washed through him.

This was a threat, a warning about what could happen.

"So someone already has smallpox?" Gunner asked. "Are we too late?"

She examined the photo more closely. "No, this probably isn't smallpox, actually. It's more likely chicken pox. The lesions are slightly different. But the message these guys are trying to send is the same: they want innocent people to suffer."

"I need to let Cassidy know about the photo," he muttered, ignoring the soft breeze that swept over him as they stood outside the front door.

There was no comfort in this situation right now. None.

Noelle grabbed his arm again, and Gunner felt that familiar shock of electricity. He ignored it.

"There's something I need to ask you first," Noelle said. "I need . . . I need to talk to someone."

He stared at her a moment, contemplating what to do.

He could call Cassidy later. Time wasn't on their side. Besides, the police chief had her hands full right now with those graves.

After a moment of thought, he nodded. "Fine. Let's talk."

Visible relief swept through Noelle's gaze.

With shaking hands, she unlocked the door and pushed it open.

Gunner took a tissue from his pocket and took the picture down. Then he gently grasped her arm and led her inside.

He gently deposited her by the wall. "Stay here. If you hear anything, run. Call 911. Understand?"

Noelle stared up at him, her lips practically quivering as she nodded. "I understand."

But her voice came out quiet and almost childlike. She was frightened—as she should be. These guys had kept her alive for a reason.

Most likely, that meant they weren't done with her yet.

Gunner checked out her house, searching under every bed and in every closet.

He paused by the mirror on her dresser and touched the cross necklace hanging there.

He sucked in a breath.

He'd given that to her when she was rescued. He'd always worn it, and she'd been so shaken that he'd wanted to reassure her.

She'd gripped the cross in her hands and risen to her feet, ready to go.

That was one of his last true moments of faith.

Now, it seemed like such a distant part of his life.

He swallowed hard, setting those memories aside as he searched the rest of her house.

Gunner didn't see anything of concern.

He kept his eyes open for any cameras or other devices that could have been left there.

He knew how these guys worked.

They had resources at their disposal, and they would use whatever means possible to get what they wanted.

Finally, he made his way back to Noelle. "It's clear."

She didn't even try to hide her relief at his announcement.

"Thank you." But her voice cracked as she said the words.

Their stress wasn't over yet.

Now it was time for them to talk.

SEVENTEEN

NOELLE COULDN'T RISK anyone overhearing what she had to say. What if these guys had planted bugs in her house?

That's why she took Gunner's hand and led him down the hallway.

Confusion flashed through his gaze, but he didn't ask any questions.

Not even when she led him inside the bathroom and shut the door.

Then she turned the shower on at full blast. She pulled up something on her phone and, a moment later, soft music played through the tiny speakers. She left the device on the counter before turning toward Gunner.

She leaned against the sink, still feeling shaken and unable to get the images out of her mind.

Gunner stood close. Noelle was all too aware of his hulking presence. The bathroom wasn't that large, and there was nowhere else for him to stand.

"You don't want anyone to hear." A touch of admiration stretched through his voice.

Noelle nodded and pushed a strand of hair behind her ear. "No one can know what I'm telling you."

His gaze tightened. "What's going on?"

She swallowed hard, knowing that after she started talking, it would be too late to turn back. She wouldn't be able to undo what she had said.

Was she really prepared for this?

She wasn't sure.

Noelle raked both hands through her hair, her inner torment almost more than she could bear.

"I worked a while for Vitality Labs in France. Everyone thinks of the company as simply a cosmetics lab. Since I'm a board-certified dermatologist, it made sense that I worked there. But there was much more to it than people think."

"Okay . . ." Gunner squinted as if uncertain where she was going with this.

"I'm also a disease control expert who specializes in viruses of the skin. When I accepted this job with Vitality, they wanted me to research Staphylococcal Scalded Skin Syndrome. They hired me to be the lead researcher."

"What is Scalded Skin Syndrome?" A knot of confusion formed between his eyes.

"It's a serious infection that causes peeling skin over large parts of the body. It looks like the skin has been scalded or burned by hot liquid. It can be very painful and dangerous."

"I've never heard of it."

"It mostly affects children." Her voice cracked.

"Okay . . . how does that connect with the Alphas?" Gunner searched her gaze for the truth.

A lump formed in Noelle's throat.

She'd come this far. She knew she needed to share the rest of her story—even if she felt as if she might throw up.

Her gaze locked on Gunner's. "I'm not sure. But I keep having these flashbacks."

"What kind of flashbacks?"

"Ones that don't make any sense. They're things I don't remember . . . that don't seem real."

"Things like what?"

"You mentioned seeing a lab?" She pressed her lips together with apprehension.

"That's right."

"I don't remember seeing one . . . but I keep having visions of one. In Moscow."

"What? Anything else?"

She dragged her gaze up to meet his. "And I keep seeing my friend Bartholomew being killed . . . in front of me . . . even though I have no recollection of that happening.

———

Gunner remembered the lab he'd seen when Noelle was rescued. The equipment there had been advanced and high tech—surprising for such an old, rundown building where she was being kept.

Had the Alphas wanted Noelle and her colleagues to create a biological weapon for them? Something that could most likely harm millions.

He glanced at Noelle as steam rose around them, fogging up the mirror. The steady spray of water somehow seemed to compliment the soft music playing on her phone.

But suddenly, he felt too close to her. His skin felt too warm.

As he glanced at Noelle, her amber-colored eyes drew him in. The softly sculpted features of her face practically beckoned him to wisp his fingers across them. Her lips . . . he wanted to know what they tasted like.

None of those things were a good idea.

Gunner took a step back as he composed himself, unable to ignore the burst of attraction he felt toward her.

Developing feelings for Noelle would only end in disaster.

Acting on impulses would create confusion.

She swallowed hard—so hard that Gunner wondered if she'd felt the same spark he did.

It didn't matter.

Only keeping her safe mattered.

"What if these guys abducted you and your colleagues so you could create a strain of smallpox?" he suggested. "What if they set up a lab so you could do so?"

"Why wouldn't I remember that?"

"Amnesia?"

"It seems like they would have found me and killed me by now if that was the case. I mean, if I'm the one who made it then I could tell people what I'd done."

"Unless you were interrupted before you could finish. That would explain why they don't want you dead now."

She rubbed her temples. "If I had amnesia . . . wouldn't I know it? I mean, I have so many memories of my time in captivity. It seems I wouldn't recall anything about that time."

"I don't know the ins and outs of this, but I think this is our best theory until those memories start to emerge." He shifted. "The psychologist Ty had come out to Hope House . . . her name is Dr. Samantha Reynolds. She lives on the island. Maybe you could talk with her, and she'll have some ideas."

"I'm open to that, but . . ." Her gaze locked with his. "If I'm right . . . then this is terrible, Gunner."

Gunner studied her gaze as he searched for the truth, for more answers. "Certainly, there are other scientists out there who can do this. Not that I want anyone in this position, but I'm still trying to figure out why they're focusing so much on you."

"I'm one of the leading infectious disease specialists in the world, and one of the few that also has an emphasis in dermatology. Considering the fact that smallpox starts as blisters on the skin . . ."

"I see." Realization washed over him. "You have unique talents."

Her gaze flittered up to his. "I don't know what to do."

Gunner searched his thoughts as he tried to come up with an answer.

He wasn't sure there was one.

But he knew the stakes were higher than ever.

CHAPTER
EIGHTEEN

STILL IN THE bathroom with steam filling the air, Noelle stared at the photo that had been left on her door and felt another shiver of fear race down her spine.

She was in trouble. No one could deny that.

But she had no idea what to do.

Gunner didn't either, though why would she expect him to?

This was her problem. And the solution wouldn't be easy.

Suddenly, she didn't feel as if she'd be safe anywhere.

"You shouldn't stay here at your house alone." Gunner glanced around her bathroom as he made the statement, his muscles hardening as if he were on duty. "It's not secure."

Her thoughts exactly. But what other choice did she have? She couldn't stay with Rachel and put her friend in danger. Where else would she go?

Nowhere. She had nowhere else to stay.

"I'll be fine." Her voice wavered, belying her apprehension.

His expression remained terse. "No, you won't. Even if these guys don't want you dead, who's to say they won't grab you again and try to force you to do something for them? And when they're done with you, they'll kill you and maybe your mom as well."

Noelle reeled at his words—but only for a moment before collecting herself. "Aren't you full of good news?"

Gunner shifted. "I'm just trying to be realistic here. This is bigger than you and your mom, though. You have to know that."

"I do. But I don't know what I'm supposed to do." Noelle raked a hand through her hair again. "And I have no idea how to figure this situation out and how to do the right thing—or what the right thing even is."

"For now, come stay at Hope House."

She considered the idea a moment before saying, "I can't do that. I wouldn't want to impose."

"I'm sure it will be fine. We need to call Cassidy anyway. I'll talk to her and Ty. But I know they're always willing to help out someone in need."

Noelle wasn't sure how she felt about staying at the house. If she was there, at least she'd be around two former Navy SEALs and the police chief. But Faith was also there, and Noelle didn't like the idea of putting the little girl in danger.

But maybe only Noelle and her mom were in danger. That's how it seemed at least.

Then she remembered today's discoveries. The disturbed graves. The possibility of smallpox.

No, it appeared the world at large might be in danger also.

Finally, she nodded. "Let's talk to Cassidy and see what she and Ty say. But if they're not comfortable, then—"

"Then they'll recommend somewhere else for you to stay," Gunner finished. "These guys know what they're doing. I promise you that."

Noelle nodded again, resigning herself to that idea. She didn't have any better ones. "Okay then. Let's talk to Cassidy."

"I'll give her a call. Pack a bag to take with you in the meantime . . . just in case."

Gunner watched as Ty showed Noelle to her room at Ty and Cassidy's place, one right across the hall from where he was staying.

He'd originally been staying in one of the cabanas outside. But with Noelle being here, he wanted to be close—just in case she needed him.

She asked for a few minutes alone to unwind but promised to be out soon.

Gunner and Ty walked downstairs together. It was

already dark outside. The day had been long, and his body was growing weary.

Cassidy wasn't home yet, and Ty had just put Faith down for the night.

This was the perfect opportunity for the two of them to chat.

Gunner turned to Ty and lowered his voice. "I'd personally like to keep an eye on Noelle."

"That's a good idea." Ty rubbed his jaw as he nodded. "If she agrees."

Gunner would need to convince Noelle to agree.

But another thought filled his head almost as quickly. At one time, Gunner had been more than capable of defending others. But what if that wasn't the case now?

His heart pounded in his ears at the haunting thought.

Would it be better if someone else watched her back?

"Gunner?"

His gaze met Ty's. "What if I can't protect her?"

Ty's expression remained steady, without so much as a hint of doubt. "You are just as capable as anyone else. You haven't let that prosthetic hold you back yet. Why would you start now?"

Gunner rubbed his leg—the one that wasn't there anymore—and again remembered his loss. Remembered the deep-seated worry he'd felt since his world had been turned upside-down. The worry that he'd never be whole again. That he'd never be capable.

Wasn't that why Gunner had come here to Hope House? To rediscover himself and find some of that confidence he'd lost?

But it was even more than confidence he needed.

He needed to find his purpose.

He'd felt as if he'd been set adrift for two years. Maybe it was time to change that.

Gunner drew in a deep breath as he tried to sort his thoughts. He'd need some time to contend with his questions.

Then again, he'd already had so much time. But maybe he was inching closer toward accepting his new position in life and making the best of it. Unfortunately, would it take another tragedy for that to fully happen?

He glanced at Ty again as his thoughts shifted. "I'm worried about what's going on here on the island."

Ty rubbed his jaw. "Me too."

Gunner felt like he did when he'd prepared himself for battle as a SEAL.

Except this time he had no idea what he was going up against.

CHAPTER
NINETEEN

AS SOON AS Noelle heard Cassidy's voice downstairs, she hurried from her room.

She'd been listening for Cassidy to get back, desperate to hear an update on the grave situation.

Cassidy, Ty, and Gunner all stood near the front door when Noelle reached them.

"Noelle." Cassidy nodded at her, sounding a bit stiff and formal.

Noelle saw the exhaustion in Cassidy's face. No doubt this had been a long workday.

"I guess you're all waiting for an update?" Cassidy glanced at the three of them.

"You want to sit down first?" Ty pulled out a chair from the kitchen table. "I can get you something to eat if you're hungry."

Cassidy shook her head. "I'm fine. It's been a long day, but that's the nature of my job."

Noelle waited, anxious to hear any news—and to show her the photo that had been left on her door.

"First of all, if you're comfortable with it, I'd like to talk to you about those photos of your mom," Cassidy started.

"What about them?"

"She showed them to me," Ty said. "I hope that's okay. But we were able to make out some mountains in the background. I'm wondering if I get a team together, if they might be able to track her down."

"You think you'd be able to do that?"

"It's a possibility We're good at what we do. And without having your mom to leverage over you, they suddenly have no power."

Noelle nodded. "If you think you could find her . . ."

"With your permission, I'll put some of my guys on it."

"I'd appreciate that." Noelle hoped her gaze showed her gratitude. "Thank you."

"Good. I'm glad that worked out." Cassidy let out a sigh. "We haven't found the persons responsible for digging up the graves. We've talked to various people looking for witnesses. There are none."

"Did you talk to the people staying in the houses around the cemetery?" Noelle asked. She'd told Cassidy she'd seen someone inside one of them.

"There was no one suspicious—only curious vacationers wondering what was going on. The graves were most likely dug up at night when everyone was sleeping."

"Was there any other evidence left?" Gunner asked.

"We took impressions of some tire tracks, but I'm not sure how helpful they'll be." Cassidy turned to Noelle. "What else can you tell me about our earlier conversation? Has anything else come to mind?"

Noelle licked her lips as the weight of the situation pressed on her. "It's like I said—there are viruses that can survive in preserved tissues. Diseases can be brought back to life, so to speak. I can't imagine with the heat and humidity around here that bodies that old would be preserved, however."

"Based on my limited knowledge, I agree." Cassidy rubbed her face before straightening. "But why smallpox?"

"My only guess is that instead of trying to reinvent the wheel, someone could be trying to use a virus that already exists."

"Who has the capability of doing that?"

She flushed. "I suppose I could. I mean, it *is* within my field of study."

Cassidy shifted, her gaze narrowing. "What would that involve?"

"I don't have the equipment for it, if that's what you're wondering. It's a complicated set of procedures that takes time and maybe even a little bit of luck."

"Does Ocean Essence have that equipment?" Ty asked.

Noelle felt like she couldn't breathe. "Perhaps. Some of it, at least."

They all exchanged looks.

Noelle's thoughts continued to race.

Her gaze met Cassidy's again. "Did you happen to look into those graves that were dug up? Did you find out what those people died from? That could give you your answer right there."

"We requested the records from the county. We should know by tomorrow."

"If it comes back that they did die of smallpox . . ." Noelle started.

Cassidy frowned. "Then I'll have to call the CDC. This could become a national emergency situation."

———

Cassidy's head spun.

What did all of this mean when she combined it with everything that had been happening here on the island? Could Russian terrorists have come here to abduct Noelle?

But they had the chance to do that and didn't.

Did they plan to use the equipment at Ocean Essence for their purposes?

Or were they sending a message about what they were planning?

But why send out a warning?

Nothing made sense.

"Thanks for sharing," Cassidy finally told Noelle. A burst of exhaustion seemed to hit her, and she closed her eyes. "You know what? Maybe I should sit after all."

Ty pulled out a chair for her, and she lowered herself there.

The rest of them followed suit, and they all gathered at the kitchen table.

"The good news is, if these men still need my expertise, then they haven't developed anything yet," Noelle said.

"Maybe that is good news." Cassidy's gaze met Noelle's. "Maybe you should just stay put for a while. Not even go to work. This is a serious situation."

"If I do that, these people will know something is up." Noelle rubbed her arms as if chilly. "I can't break my routine, or they'll become suspicious. And my mom . . ."

"You're right," Cassidy said. "We're making a lot of assumptions right now. We need proof before we move forward."

"But what if the only proof we find happens when it's too late?" Ty asked.

Silence stretched between them.

She didn't like that possibility.

"It's like Noelle said—if they're trying to manipulate her into doing their dirty deeds, then there shouldn't be a direct threat yet. But we need to be on guard and be ready to act. The implications of this . . ." Cassidy's voice drifted.

"So until we know something for sure, I continue on as normal?" Noelle asked. "Pretend like everything is routine?"

"Yes. And we keep an eye on you in the meantime."

"I can drive you to work and pick you up." Gunner's deep voice cut through the air. "I'd feel better if someone was with you at all times."

"Won't that look suspicious though?" Noelle asked.

Cassidy turned toward Gunner and narrowed her gaze with thought. "Do you think they know you were one of the SEALs who rescued her?"

Gunner shrugged. "I don't think my identity was compromised. It was supposed to be top secret. Then again, a lot of things are supposed to be."

Cassidy couldn't argue with that point. "I think it's a good idea if you have someone watching your back."

But Noelle still looked uncertain as she frowned and shrugged. "You don't think that these guys are going to be suspicious if they see Gunner and me together?"

Cassidy's thoughts raced. "Not if they think there's a good reason for it."

"Like what?" Noelle sounded earnestly confused.

"Not if they think . . . I don't know." Cassidy shrugged. "Not if they think the two of you are dating."

Noelle and Gunner exchanged a look.

Cassidy wasn't sure exactly how they would react to that statement. But that scenario made the most sense. It was the best reason for the two of them to be seen together, especially if these guys didn't know Gunner was one of the SEALs involved with her rescue.

This situation was tenuous at best. They needed to be wise with every decision.

Because Cassidy didn't want any more dead bodies on this island.

There had already been too many.

Not only that . . . but this had the potential to reach further than Lantern Beach.

This had the potential to become a worldwide threat.

CHAPTER
TWENTY

GUNNER TOSSED and turned in bed, unable to sleep. He had too much on his mind. And his phantom leg pain continued.

The sensation drove him crazy. He was a logical person. He knew his leg was no longer there.

So why did it still hurt so badly sometimes? His doctor said the pain could last for years. But the aches were just reminders of his brokenness.

Finally, Gunner couldn't take it anymore.

He climbed out of bed and slipped on his prosthetic. Then he quietly crept downstairs. He'd get a glass of water and see if that helped.

At least the liquid would cool off the sweat that had spread across his skin.

As soon as he stepped down the stairs, he spotted someone on the couch.

He tensed, readying himself for trouble.

Then Noelle's face came into view.

Based on her wide eyes, she looked just as surprised as he felt.

She sat on the couch with her legs curled under her and a cup of something warm on the table beside her. Her Bible lay open in her lap.

"Sorry." He took a step back. "I didn't mean to interrupt."

She shifted before saying in a soft voice, "No, please stay. I couldn't sleep."

"I couldn't either." He headed to the kitchen and grabbed a glass of water, unsure if he should take it back to his room or stay out here.

Part of him wanted to use this opportunity to talk to Noelle more. Maybe it would be better if the two of them weren't total strangers, especially if they had any hopes of pulling off the idea that they could be dating.

After a moment of hesitation, he sat down on the other end of the couch and took a long sip of his drink.

He then set the glass on a coaster on the table and turned to her. "How are you holding up?"

"As well as can be imagined." Noelle shrugged, but an edge of defeat had entered her voice. "These moments when our lives are turned upside-down can really define us."

"You think so?"

"I do. Anyone can persist during the good times. But it takes strength to persevere when everything goes south."

He nodded slowly before saying, "Blessed is the one who perseveres under trial because, having stood the test, that person will receive the crown of life that the Lord has promised to those who love him. James 1:12."

"One of my favorite Bible verses." She shifted to better face him. "And one you obviously know well."

"I do. You speak as if you know all about preserving. Are you talking about when you were abducted?"

Sadness filled her gaze. "Partly. But, believe it or not, that wasn't the hardest time of my life."

Questions scurried through his mind. Then what was? What could possibly be harder than that?

He didn't ask. She'd share if she wanted.

Instead, Gunner rubbed his leg again as that phantom pain returned. Every time he felt it, it reminded him of what he'd lost.

"Are you okay?" Noelle's eyes narrowed as she studied him.

He forced himself to relax his expression. "I'm fine."

But one look at Noelle's face, and he knew that she didn't believe him.

———

"I can only imagine how difficult it must be to lose a limb," Noelle started, casually leaning back onto the couch.

She'd been obsessing over smallpox since she sat down. She'd been praying. Seeking answers. Trying to sort her thoughts.

But she'd gotten nowhere so far.

Now her thoughts turned toward Gunner. She could use a mental break anyway.

And she had so many questions for him, so much she wanted to say.

However, she knew she was treading in personal—and possibly unwelcome—territory with Gunner. Maybe she shouldn't.

But losing his leg had to be such a huge challenge for him.

Life had thrown him a curveball. More than a curveball. No doubt he grieved over what he'd lost—as would anyone in his situation.

The question was: had his grief broken him?

"I'm fine." Gunner's voice sounded stiff as he looked away.

Noelle didn't believe him. Instead, she scooted across the couch toward him. "If you don't mind me asking, what happened exactly? How did you lose your leg? I know it happened during the rescue, but how?"

Gunner's face tightened. "I don't like to talk about it."

"It must have happened right after you rescued me. Was it from the explosion I saw?" She hadn't been able to stop thinking about it ever since he told her.

He said nothing.

Noelle's heart pounded harder. She knew whatever had happened wasn't directly her fault. But she couldn't help but marvel that Gunner had made this sacrifice because of her.

She reached across the chasm between them and squeezed his arm, forgetting her resolve not to touch him again. He needed human contact. Needed to know he wasn't alone. Needed to know his efforts weren't in vain.

"Thank you," she nearly whispered.

Noelle fully expected Gunner to pull away.

He didn't.

"You're welcome." Gunner's voice sounded gruff with emotion, and his gaze clouded. It almost seemed as if his mind had been swept back in time—back to his worst nightmares.

"I guess to say your life has been turned upside-down would be an understatement." Noelle didn't know why she kept pushing.

She sensed Gunner needed to talk, that he still hadn't come to terms with his loss, with his grief. She knew what that was like. She'd been through it.

The circumstances had been different. The loss was different.

But the pain was the same.

She'd fought her way back to the surface, and so could he.

"It's not important." Gunner shrugged her question off, looking more irritated by the moment.

"I know your first inclination might be that you have to be strong all the time. But you don't."

"You don't know what you're saying." His gaze darkened. "I said I don't want to talk about it. Understand?"

Noelle knew by the firmness in his words that she'd crossed the line.

"I understand." She withdrew and scooted back closer to her mug of herbal tea. She took a long sip before standing. "I'm going to drink the rest of this in my room. I hope you have a good night."

Before she could overstep anymore, she grabbed her Bible and went upstairs.

But Noelle wished more than anything that she had the ability to take away some of Gunner's pain.

However, she couldn't do that. There was only one who could.

And it wasn't Gunner either.

It was God.

CHAPTER
TWENTY-ONE

NOELLE BARELY SLEPT the rest of the night.

At least she hadn't slept until about four a.m. That was the last time she remembered looking at the clock beside her bed.

The next thing she knew, her alarm began beeping and pulled her from a deep sleep at 6:30.

She scrambled out of bed and quickly took a shower.

She dreaded going downstairs and possibly running into Gunner again.

He must resent her for overstepping last night.

Perhaps it had been the stress of the day playing on her emotions. But it was none of her business what happened to him, and she shouldn't have brought the subject up or pretended to understand.

The good news was that they *had* made strides forward. However, they'd also taken steps back. Things already felt tenuous between them, but now she knew they'd be worse.

It was a delicate dance, it seemed.

Noelle walked into the empty kitchen and inhaled the scent of fresh coffee. Kujo wandered over, and Noelle rubbed his head. Maybe she should get a dog. It was nice to see a friendly face in the morning.

She spotted a note on the counter and read it. The masculine handwriting instructed her to help herself to both the coffee and some muffins that had been placed in a basket on the counter. Ty had left this, if she had to guess.

Noelle could only assume that Cassidy and Ty were already at work. She knew Ty's parents lived next door and helped them take care of Faith. She'd met the couple at church and then again at the cookout.

She grabbed a blueberry muffin and took a bite, marveling at how surprisingly tasty it was. Then she poured herself a cup of coffee and added a splash of cream.

She glanced at her watch. She needed to be at work in half an hour, which meant she'd need to leave within the next fifteen or so minutes. Her bruises were darker today, but the swelling on her face had gone down some. She'd done her best to cover up her injuries with makeup, but every time she smiled or widened her eyes, her face hurt.

The pain was a reminder about what had happened.

About what *had* happened.

Everything so far this morning had seemed so

mundane, so normal.

But nothing about today would be normal.

Especially if the Alphas had their way.

She'd thought about the situation all night.

The only comfort she had was in realizing these men hadn't completed anything yet. And Noelle wouldn't help them do so.

She'd die first.

She could practically hear the clock ticking in her head.

Noelle had to take that threat seriously.

She finished her muffin and drank her last drop of coffee. She was just setting the cup in the sink when she heard someone coming down the stairs.

Regret filled her when she saw Gunner approaching. He'd already dressed in some black cargo pants and a white Riptide Surf Shop T-shirt that nicely displayed his broad chest. His hair was still wet as if he'd just gotten out of the shower.

He looked . . . handsome.

Then again, she'd always thought he looked handsome.

"Morning," Gunner muttered as he paused on the opposite side of the breakfast bar.

He never sounded especially friendly, but right now he *especially* didn't sound friendly. Was it because of their conversation last night?

It had to be.

More regret filled her. She'd overstepped. She knew better.

"Morning." Noelle hesitantly crept closer, every action feeling burdened. "Listen, you don't have to drive me to work. I'm sure you have other things to do, and this whole plan where we pretend we're dating is ridiculous—"

"I want to." But his voice sounded hard as he said the words. He hurried around the bar, reached past her, and grabbed a muffin. "I can take this to go. Are you ready?"

Noelle raised her eyebrows, unsure how to read him. How were they ever going to pretend to be dating?

But finally, she nodded. She hated how self-conscious she felt around him this morning, but she understood why.

"One more thing before we leave," Gunner started.

"What's that?"

He pulled something from his pocket. It was a small ring—too small for her fingers. "Could you wear this?"

"Is it a . . . toe ring?"

He nodded. "If you're wearing sneakers, no one will notice it—unlike a necklace, ring, or earrings."

"But why?"

"It has a tracker on it. I'd feel better if I had a means to find you, just in case . . ."

Her throat tightened. "I see. Good idea. You just happened to have one of these on hand?"

A slight smile feathered across his lips. "Not exactly. But Ty and his guys did. They said we can borrow it. It's already set up, so as long as you're wearing it, we'd be able to find you."

"Okay then. I'll put it on in the car."

She was wearing heels today, so they would be easy to slip off.

The two of them awkwardly left the house, and Noelle locked it behind them.

A moment later, they climbed inside Gunner's Jeep and started down the road. Noelle checked her emails as they rode instead of talking. There was no need to force polite conversation.

Gunner seemed like the type who needed space when he was feeling troubled—and who hung onto his grumpiness.

Her ex-husband had always said Noelle spent too much time trying to change people. To help others.

Maybe he was right.

Finally, she and Gunner pulled up to Ocean Essence.

And not a moment too soon. Noelle wasn't sure how much longer she could take the tension between them.

She quickly turned toward Gunner, anxious for some space. "Thanks for the ride."

"You should call me when you're about fifteen minutes away from leaving." Gunner sounded serious and all business. "I'll come and pick you up. Or if you go to lunch or something, call me then too."

Noelle didn't like the idea of having to do that. She planned on eating at the office today. She could order food from one of the nearby restaurants since she'd forgotten to pack anything.

She started to open the door when Gunner touched her arm.

Electricity zapped through her again, and her heart rate quickened.

What was she doing? She couldn't give a second thought to those feelings. Not if she were smart.

"If we want this ruse to work, then you should probably give me a hug," he murmured.

Realization washed over her. That was right. The two of them needed to at least look like they were interested in each other if they wanted anyone to buy their story.

Noelle forced herself to move toward him and wrap her arms around his neck.

As she did, the scent of Gunner's minty cologne filled her nostrils.

Something about the embrace made Noelle's heart race even faster, and her thoughts suddenly felt scrambled.

Quickly, she pulled away before Gunner could see how much the action had affected her.

She exited the Jeep. As she did, she nearly stumbled over the curb before finally heading up the sidewalk. *Get with it, Noelle!*

Her cheeks heated.

She straightened her black pencil skirt, hoping Gunner hadn't seen her clumsiness.

But she knew he had. No doubt, he'd be watching her every move until she was inside the office.

She scanned her surroundings one last time, looking for a sign that anyone—anyone besides Gunner—was watching her.

Nothing suspicious stood out.

She quickly hurried inside, thankful to have some space from the man.

———

Gunner couldn't deny that he'd felt something pass between him and Noelle.

But he couldn't let it affect him.

Besides, even if he were attracted to her, that didn't mean he had to act on it.

Keeping his distance was the only smart thing to do.

Noelle was off-limits.

She'd been off-limits when he rescued her two years ago. Not only because she'd been a part of an operation, but Gunner had also been dating Laura at that time.

But after he and Laura had split, Gunner had thought about Noelle on more than one occasion.

She had a kindness about her that was unusual. And fascinating.

She'd been scared, but she'd still had a fire in her.

She'd been unwilling to leave without her colleague.

And when she'd looked at Gunner, it was almost like they'd known each other for years. Like she could see inside him. Like they connected in an unusual, unexplainable way.

Gunner knew he'd been gruff with her last night, and he regretted that. He should have apologized this morning for snapping at her, but he thought maybe it was better if he didn't.

Noelle's personal questions added contention between them, but maybe that was for the best. They shouldn't get too close. They needed to concentrate on the threat against her—on the threat against humanity. That was their first priority.

Yet, Gunner could see he'd made her feel self-conscious, and he hadn't intended on doing that.

No, what he wanted to do was to hug her again and smell the fresh scent of her cotton-scented shampoo. To feel her soft skin against him.

But that was a big fat bad idea.

He scanned the area around the two-story modern office building in the distance. It was secluded and surrounded by marshes, creating a peaceful setting. He supposed that was what the company's leadership wanted—for their employees to be inspired by nature and the beach.

Gunner didn't want to leave this parking lot. If he had his way, he'd stay all day to try to keep an eye on Noelle.

But he couldn't do that. As long as she stayed safe inside the office, she should be okay. Only people with security clearances could get into the actual laboratory, from what he understood. And the company had hired a security guard from Blackout to patrol outside at all times of the day.

Noelle should be safe inside.

Gunner scanned his surroundings one more time, but he didn't see anything worrisome.

Before he could back out, his phone rang. He hit the

button to answer it through his vehicle's Bluetooth.

It was Commander Ford.

After a few minutes of banalities, Gunner got to the point. "Have you heard anything about the Alphas lately?"

A beat passed. "The Alphas? Didn't expect you to be asking about them. Why? Did they pop back up on your radar?"

"I'd rather not say right now. I'm trying to ascertain whether or not I should be concerned."

"Anything with the Alphas, you should be concerned about." His voice sounded dead serious.

Gunner's jaw tightened before he asked his next question. "Was there anything about my last mission that you didn't tell me?"

"What do you mean?"

"I mean, I realize information is on a need-to-know basis. But some things have come to light recently . . . and I feel like my team and I were put in a situation that was far more deadly than anyone ever let on."

"You know how these things work. That's what you do as a SEAL. You follow orders."

Gunner couldn't argue with Ford's words. But he'd trusted his commander. Trusted that Ford wouldn't purposefully send Gunner's guys somewhere knowing they could be killed.

"Is there anything you couldn't tell me then that you can tell me now?" he repeated.

Gunner waited for the commander's response.

CHAPTER
TWENTY-TWO

AS SOON AS Noelle reached her office, Rachel slipped inside and shut the door.

"Are you okay?" Rachel rushed as concern laced her voice.

Noelle should have called her friend earlier. But with everything going on, it had slipped her mind.

"I'm fine," Noelle insisted, trying to play down yesterday's events.

"What's going on, Noelle?" Rachel stared at her, waiting for an answer.

What Noelle wouldn't do to be able to tell her friend everything. But that would only put Rachel in danger. She couldn't do that.

She licked her lips before saying, "I wish I could tell you. Not to sound cliché . . . but it's complicated."

"I understand complicated." Rachel stared at her another moment, questions in her gaze. "I have to get to a meeting now. But we need to talk later."

Noelle frowned. There was so much she couldn't say.

At least she'd bought herself some time. She hated to keep her friend in the dark. She and Rachel had become close fast, and she wanted to be honest with her.

Nearly as soon as Rachel left, Noelle's cell phone rang, and a name she hadn't seen in a long time appeared on her screen.

She almost didn't answer. The last thing she needed in her life was any more drama. And she wasn't in the mood for small talk.

But she answered anyway.

"Noelle?" Josh's deep voice stretched through the line.

He hadn't only been her husband. He'd also been a colleague. Now, he was the head research scientist at the Ocean Essence laboratory up in Baltimore.

"Hey there." She softened her voice.

She didn't hate her ex. Really, she felt sorry for him. They both had a lot of regrets.

"What's going on?"

"I wanted you to hear this from me."

Instantly, concern filled her. Something was wrong. Why else would Josh call?

"What's going on?" She leaned back in her chair as she braced herself for more bad news.

"It's about Thomas."

Her breath caught. Thomas was her fellow scientist who'd been abducted with her.

"What about him?" Noelle hadn't stayed in touch with him.

In fact, the two of them seemed to remind each other of the horrific things that had happened when they'd been abducted. Not talking had seemed like a better option than remembering.

"I was just watching the local news up here." Josh's voice tightened. "Noelle, I don't know how to say this. But Thomas is . . . dead."

———

Gunner kept thinking about his conversation with Commander Ford.

As he did, he glanced at the woods in the distance.

Was that someone watching him?

His muscles bristled.

He wasn't seeing things.

Someone was out there.

It was time to get some answers.

He climbed from his Jeep. As he strode toward the woods, he looked for the Blackout guard.

But Titus, who was on duty today, was on the other side of the building overseeing a delivery.

Gunner didn't have time to get him.

Instead, he stepped into the woods.

But the shadow had disappeared.

That didn't deter him.

Gunner continued searching for the figure.

He paused to listen. Whoever was out there would move eventually. Gunner could wait him out.

But all he heard was the gentle breeze blowing the leaves and the marsh grass.

The watcher was doing a good job concealing himself.

Was this the man who'd beaten Noelle?

Was this man affiliated with the group that had caused Gunner to lose his leg?

Anger burned through him.

Then a stick cracked.

His senses went on alert, and he glanced around.

The noise had come from several feet away.

Gunner bristled as he wove between the trees toward that location.

He still didn't see anyone.

But this man was out there. Closer than ever.

A new sound cut through the silence.

Gunner's phone.

If the man didn't know where Gunner was before, he did now.

Gunner's muscles threaded together as he glanced around.

With the man still not in sight, he grabbed his phone and checked the screen.

It was Noelle.

Concern pulsed through him. She wasn't the type to call just to chat. No, she must have a good reason.

He quickly answered, hoping Noelle wasn't in trouble.

"Gunner . . . we need to talk," she rushed. "Now."

His breath caught when he heard the urgency in her voice. "Did something happen?"

"It's Thomas. He's . . . dead. They killed him."

Thomas Black? The man who'd been abducted along with her?

Gunner's pulse pounded harder.

Thomas's death raised so many more questions. It only confirmed that the danger around Noelle was real. That these men were willing to kill.

He cast one last glance at the woods before heading back toward Ocean Essence. "Stay where you are. I'm on my way."

Without wasting another moment, he hurried to find her.

NOELLE RUSHED OUTSIDE and spotted Gunner's Jeep.

She ran toward it.

She knew Gunner would probably tell her to wait. That he'd want to escort her to the Jeep.

But she couldn't do that.

She felt claustrophobic inside her office, and she couldn't stay there a moment longer.

As she hurried toward it, Gunner joined her.

Where had he come from?

The woods?

"What are you doing?" She glanced around, wondering what she'd missed.

"Just keeping an eye on things," he mumbled. "Let's talk more in the Jeep."

As soon as she climbed into his vehicle, Gunner opened his mouth as if he might lecture her. But he must have seen her expression and changed his mind.

She wasn't sure how it happened.

Maybe it was the compassion in his gaze. Or maybe she was simply overwhelmed.

But somehow, Noelle found herself in Gunner's arms. Found her head pressed into his chest so firmly that she could hear his heart beating strong and steady.

Had she initiated the hug, or had he?

She wasn't sure.

She only knew that having someone to hold her up felt amazing. She'd felt so alone for the past couple of years.

She hadn't even realized exactly how much.

Finally, she pulled away from him and drew in a raspy breath.

Gunner kept a hand on her shoulder as he peered at her. "Do you want to tell me what's going on? I need more details."

"Josh—my former colleague," she licked her lips as she considered also adding "my ex-husband" but changed her mind, "just called. He told me Thomas Black died in a robbery while in a convenience store."

Gunner had to know that was an unlikely story. The timing was uncanny given everything else that had happened.

"When did that happen?" His voice sounded deep and rumbling.

"Last night." Noelle's voice cracked as her haggard gaze met his. "Am I next?"

A cry slipped from her in the silence following the question.

"Hey, it's going to be okay." Gunner pulled her into another hug.

This time, Noelle melted in his embrace.

Tears flowed down her cheeks.

She couldn't believe this was happening.

If the Alphas had killed Thomas, then they'd kill her too.

Gunner didn't pull away. He let Noelle cry for as long as she needed.

But she knew she couldn't stay like this forever. When she went back to work, she'd look like a mess. Her face always got red and blotchy when she cried.

She eased back a little, and Gunner studied her expression before softly asking, "Why don't you call in sick for the rest of the day?"

Noelle considered his idea but shook her head. "I can't do that. Besides, working helps to keep my thoughts occupied. Sitting around all day just thinking about everything sounds miserable."

Gunner didn't say anything for a moment until he finally nodded. "Okay then. Let's go get something to eat instead. You need some time before you go back in there anyway. One look at you, and everyone's going to know something's wrong."

She knew there was truth behind his words.

She agreed.

But Noelle's entire world felt like it was caving in on her right now.

Gunner's thoughts raced.

Just when it seemed like the stakes couldn't get any higher, they did.

He felt personally responsible for making sure Noelle was okay. Not only that but, if Gunner were honest with himself, he was developing feelings for her.

Could there be something between them? Could romance and love be in his future? If anyone had asked him just a week ago, Gunner would have denied it.

But now he wondered if he was wrong.

Maybe he just needed the right woman in his life.

Laura had been kind. But she hadn't understood his pain. She'd lived a pampered life.

Maybe he should have given her a chance after he'd lost his leg. But the truth was, there had been issues between them anyway. On paper, they were perfect together. But in real life, something was missing. A spark maybe.

Could he have been happy with her? Absolutely.

But could he be even happier with someone else? Yes, for sure.

He scanned the area around the Ocean Essence building one more time and looked for the mystery man he'd spotted earlier.

He saw no one.

No doubt the guy was long gone.

Should he mention the incident to Noelle?

He decided not to. Not right now, at least. She was already dealing with enough stress.

Gunner put his Jeep into Reverse and drove away

from Ocean Essence. He headed down the road toward The Crazy Chefette, one of the most popular restaurants here on the island due to the chef's creative food combinations.

When they arrived, he parked and glanced around again, looking for any signs of trouble. Not seeing any, he helped Noelle out and ushered her inside. They took a table away from any windows, and a waitress brought them water right away. Noelle took several long sips as if she were dehydrated.

Gunner didn't even bother to dive into any deep conversations until after they'd ordered. Noelle went straight for comfort food—a grilled cheese and peach sandwich with homemade chips and ranch dressing. He got a burger and fries.

He glanced around and saw several people he recognized, including Hunter Bancroft, another former SEAL.

He waved hello from across the room.

Then he turned back to Noelle and waited until she was ready to talk.

"I just don't know what to do." Noelle squeezed the skin between her eyes as if she had a headache coming on.

"I can look into Thomas's death," he started. "I'll call my former commander again. We just spoke, but he didn't mention this. Maybe he doesn't know yet. Maybe he does and didn't tell me."

"If you think that would help . . ." She sounded unconvinced.

Gunner wished he had some great advice to give her. But he didn't. He only wished he could somehow make these problems magically disappear.

But a magic solution didn't exist.

The only way to get through this was to travel through it.

He let out a breath. "The best thing we can do right now is to find answers and keep you safe."

Noelle's gaze locked with his. "Is that even possible?"

Gunner knew why she asked that question. He understood why she was afraid.

They were dealing with dangerous men with innumerable resources at their disposal. The Alphas would use whatever it took to get what they wanted.

Apparently, what they wanted was Noelle.

When their food arrived, she absently began to pick at her sandwich.

"Let's just take this one step at a time, okay?" Gunner reached across the table and squeezed her hand.

She nodded, her eyes still dazed and her words nearly listless. "I wish I could be as calm as you are."

He wanted to refute Noelle's words, but he didn't. If she only knew about his struggles . . . she wouldn't have been so quick to say that. He'd even taken up boxing for a while as a way to help ease his stress.

He'd felt anything but calm.

"Gunner . . . when you rescued me from that compound in Moscow . . ."

"Yes?"

She licked her lips. "I remember it so vividly. I remember how I wanted to curl into a ball and hide instead of facing the danger of escaping. I was nearly immobilized. Then you told me, 'Fight. Fight with everything you've got inside you. Never give up.' I still think about that when I get scared." Noelle drew her gaze up to meet his, pausing with half her sandwich in her hands.

Her words resonated through him.

Gunner had no idea when he'd offered that advice that his words would stick with Noelle. But he was glad he could help. The worst thing someone could do in a tough situation was to give up.

Yet wasn't that what Gunner had done after losing his leg?

The realization felt like a slap in the face.

"You're stronger than you know." He meant his words.

Gratitude filled Noelle's gaze. "I hope so."

He shifted. "Listen, I'm sorry for getting snappy last night."

"I shouldn't have pushed—"

"It's a touchy subject, but that doesn't excuse me. I need to learn to open up more. To let down my walls. To stop keeping things bottled up inside."

"I'm always here as a listening ear if you need someone."

Their gazes remained locked, and another surge of hope swept through him. Maybe his future wasn't as bleak as he thought. Maybe the sacrifices he'd made weren't in vain.

He started to say more when the restaurant's front door opened.

Gunner felt his gaze darken when he saw Rex Houghton step inside.

Noelle followed his line of sight, and a strange expression crossed her face.

Was she interested in the guy? Gunner didn't see Rex as her type. But Gunner didn't really know Noelle that well either. Maybe he was just reading too much into it.

Besides, it didn't matter.

Even though he and Noelle had shared some moments, that didn't mean they were ready for a relationship. Or that either of them was even looking for a relationship, for that matter.

But if that was the case, why did Gunner feel his back muscles thread into knots as Rex approached their table?

CHAPTER
TWENTY-FOUR

NOELLE WASN'T in the mood to talk to Rex.

He was a nice enough guy. There was nothing not to like about him. He was good-looking, kind, successful.

She *should* be flattered by his attention. She'd even considered going out with him again to get to know him better.

But she also felt like some sort of connection was missing, something she couldn't put her finger on or really define.

It was just something she felt.

As a scientist that said a lot.

In her line of work, she relied on testing. On logic. On evidence that she could see with her eyes.

But what Noelle was talking about right now was none of those things.

She always told herself that the heart couldn't be trusted. Wasn't that what the Bible said in Jeremiah 19 after all? *The heart is deceitful above all things and beyond cure. Who can understand it?*

People always said follow your heart. Live your best life. Go for your dreams.

But so many of those things went against what the Bible said.

"How are you doing?" Rex paused by the table, barely giving a glance to Gunner.

"Just fine," Noelle muttered, trying to keep their conversation polite.

If she were honest with herself, something about talking with Rex in front of Gunner made her uncomfortable.

The reaction didn't make sense.

Gunner had made it clear he wasn't interested in her. That was for the best. She had enough complications in her life right now.

"This island has a totally different feel in June than it did even a month ago, doesn't it?" Rex started, sounding as easygoing as ever. "There are so many people here."

"I've heard this is just the start of it," Noelle said. "July Fourth is when it peaks."

"I can't imagine the streets getting any busier. I suppose this island wasn't set up knowing so many tourists would flood here."

"It wasn't." This wasn't what Noelle wanted to talk about. It seemed so mundane.

Noelle glanced at her watch, desperate for an excuse

to leave. "You know what, I have got to get back to work. I just need to run to the bathroom first."

With that, she hurried from the table.

———

Gunner wasn't sure why Rex wasn't leaving.

Clearly, the man was only here to talk to Noelle.

But even after Noelle disappeared into the bathroom, he lingered beside the booth.

Gunner stared up at him, trying to hide his irritation.

As their gazes met, Gunner saw something in his eyes.

A smugness? Most likely.

This guy clearly had something else to say.

As if on cue, Rex leaned closer and lowered his voice. "I know what you're doing. I can see the look in your eyes."

"I don't know what you're talking about," Gunner muttered.

"Noelle needs a real man." Rex sent him a pointed look. "A *whole* man."

He glanced at Gunner's leg. His missing leg.

Anger shot through Gunner, and his hands fisted.

He'd like nothing more than to give this man a piece of his mind.

Maybe more than that.

Instead, Gunner stood, towering at least four inches above Rex.

"I don't think I asked for your opinion." His words came out louder than he'd intended.

Several people from the surrounding tables quieted to watch them.

"I just don't want you to get . . . *hurt*." Rex said the word as if Gunner were a weakling. "To become any more damaged than you already are."

"I don't think you know Noelle well enough to say what she wants or what she doesn't want, nor do you know me at all."

Rex smirked. "Are you sure about that? You don't think I know about the counseling you've been through? The PTSD you've struggled with? How you almost gave up?"

A low growl escaped from deep inside Gunner. He wanted to show this guy—

"Hey, guys." Hunter stepped between them.

Gunner hardly heard him.

Instead, he glared at Rex as he tried to keep his emotions under control.

Easier said than done.

The restaurant grew even quieter.

"Is everything okay?" a soft voice asked.

Gunner looked over and saw Noelle standing beside them, a look of confusion on her face.

He stepped back and tried to soften his shoulders. The last thing he wanted was to frighten her.

"Everything's fine." His voice sounded strained as he said the words.

"Just fine," Rex echoed as he took a step back. "I was just leaving."

With that, the man turned on his heel, picked up a to-go order on the counter, then sauntered from the restaurant as if nothing had happened.

Not until the man was out of sight did Gunner turn toward Noelle then Hunter. "Everything is fine."

"You sure about that?" Hunter locked gazes with him, questions lingering in his eyes.

Gunner shrugged off his anger. "Rex was trying to get under my skin."

"It looks like it worked." Hunter raised his eyebrows.

Instead of responding, Gunner glanced at Noelle, suddenly ready to get out of here. The whole place felt too small, too hot.

"Are you ready to go?" he asked.

She nodded.

Gunner dropped some money on the table then headed toward the door.

He hated that he'd caused a scene.

But Rex had been trying to provoke him. Gunner was grateful things hadn't gone any further than they had.

Once he and Noelle were back in his Jeep, she turned to him. Her brow was furrowed with confusion. "What happened back there?"

Gunner remembered Rex's words. *She needs a real man. A whole man.*

Initially, he'd felt a burst of indignation. Maybe even resentment.

But now the words settled in his mind, he wondered . . . what if Rex was right?

TWENTY-FIVE

THE REST of the ride back to Ocean Essence was quiet.

Gunner hadn't offered any information on that conversation with Rex. Noelle only knew he was upset about something.

She wished he would open up.

But she could only imagine what Rex might have said. The man was a little too full of himself sometimes. His success seemed to have gone to his head.

Whatever it was, Gunner seemed more distant than ever.

Then they arrived back at her work, and she paused with her hand on the door as she turned to Gunner in the Jeep. "Thank you for lunch. I appreciate it."

"Of course." He muttered, that same grumpy look in his gaze. "I'll be here as soon as you're ready to leave."

"Are you sure?" She still hated to put him out like this.

"I'm positive."

With one more lingering glance at him, Noelle slipped from his Jeep and headed toward the building.

Again, she felt relief sweep over her as soon as the door to Ocean Essence closed behind her and she was safe inside.

Kari, the receptionist, looked up and smiled politely. "Dr. Purdy . . . you just missed a visitor about twenty minutes ago."

Noelle's shoulders instantly tensed, and she was all too aware of the sound of her heart beating in her ears. "A visitor?"

"It was a man I've never seen before. But he said he needed to talk to you about some business." Kari shrugged, as cheerful as always.

What Noelle wouldn't do to have a touch of that happy-go-lucky spirit.

Instead, her blood went cold.

Had the man who'd been after her actually come to Noelle's work? Was he that brazen? That certain that Noelle had no power against him and no choice except to do exactly what he wanted?

Maybe that was true.

Either way, it didn't make her feel any better.

"Listen, could you get me an image of what this guy looks like?" she asked.

Kari frowned. "I suppose I could pull one from the security footage. It will take me a few minutes, however."

"That would be helpful." Thankfully, Kari didn't ask any more questions.

Noelle tried to put on a placid expression as she hurried to her office. The last thing she wanted was any of her coworkers to ask her questions.

She closed the door when she was inside then sagged against her desk.

What was she going to do?

As she tried to pull herself together, her phone buzzed.

She hesitated a moment before looking at the screen.

When she did, she saw it was another picture of . . . her mom. This time she stood on a secluded mountain bridge . . . close to the edge . . . appearing oblivious about the danger she faced.

Panic filled her.

These guys clearly wanted to send Noelle a message.

They were well aware of what she was doing.

Would her mom pay the price?

———

Gunner called Commander Ford again, and his former superior picked up on the first ring this time.

"What's going on now?" His voice sounded gruff.

Gunner shifted as he sat in the driver's seat of his Jeep outside the Ocean Essence office. "Thomas Black is dead."

Silence stretched a moment. "What?"

"I just found out. Did you know anything about it?"

"This is news to me."

"Something is going on," Gunner continued.

"What do you mean?"

"I think someone sold us out. That the Alphas knew we were coming and wanted to teach us a lesson. You know more than you're letting on." He'd never voiced his theory aloud before. But not any longer. This needed to be said.

Another moment of silence stretched. "Some of that information is classified."

"What if some of that information is coming into play again?" Gunner had to be careful what he said. What if he couldn't trust his commander?

The thought hit him like a ton of bricks.

But it was a possibility he needed to consider—especially if there really was a mole.

"If you know something, you need to tell me," Ford said.

His spine stiffened. "I know Thomas is dead, and someone appears to be following Dr. Noelle Purdy. I can't imagine that's a coincidence. Did something happen to Thomas before he died? Was he missing for a certain time period?"

"I honestly don't know."

The man sounded sincere but . . . "You should find out."

"Are you giving me orders, Captain?"

"Respectfully, someone needs to take this seriously.

You're in a position to find out more information than I can."

The commander remained silent several seconds before finally sighing. "Fine. I'll look into it."

"We don't have any time to waste," Gunner reminded him.

"I know. And I will say this," the commander added, "no matter where Dr. Purdy is, she's in danger."

NOELLE HEARD someone knock at her door and turned to see Rachel there.

One look at her, and her friend seemed to instantly know that something was wrong. Without invitation, Rachel slipped into the office, shut the door, and then sat in the chair across from Noelle's desk.

"Okay, my meeting is finally over. Now what's going on?" Rachel stared at Noelle, worry written in the lines of her forehead. "I can't stop thinking about how upset you looked when you left with Cassidy yesterday. That's not to mention the fact that some stranger beat you up. Now you're as pale as a ghost."

Noelle's head spun as she considered her words. How much could she say? Anything?

She wasn't sure.

Finally, she settled on, "I was actually taken hostage two years ago and held in Russia."

Rachel's eyes widened. "I remember hearing something about that on the news. You and two other guys? I mean, I didn't realize it was you."

"That was me. I thought the ordeal was behind me. But it appears some of the men who kidnapped me are on this island now, and they want to finish what they started."

Rachel's eyes grew even larger. "What? What do they want?"

Noelle wet her lips, knowing that this was where it got dicey. There were just some things she couldn't say.

"I'm not sure. But you know those graves that were disturbed on the island yesterday?"

Rachel nodded, her shoulders and neck appearing tense. "Yes. I heard about them."

"I wonder if they have anything to do with this."

Her eyes widened. "Why would that have anything to do with you?"

She shifted. "That's what I'm trying to figure out."

Noelle spent the rest of the afternoon trying to focus on work, but it was hard to concentrate with everything that had been going on.

Before Noelle knew it, her whole workday had passed, and it was time to go home.

Well, not home. But to Ty and Cassidy's place.

If Noelle could, right now she would run. Fast and furious. She wouldn't stop until she was far away from this place and completely alone where no one could find her.

But if she did that, then these guys could hurt her mom. Noelle couldn't risk that.

For that reason, she called Gunner and asked him to pick her up.

She needed to fill him in on what had happened.

While she waited, she asked Kari for a screenshot of the man who'd come asking about her. She'd made up an excuse about an ex-boyfriend. That would raise the least amount of questions.

Kari complied and handed her a print of the image.

As Noelle stared at the picture of the man, her blood went cold again.

———

Cassidy stood on the boardwalk with Ty, a cup of iced coffee in her hand. She leaned against the railing overlooking the ocean and let the salty breeze kiss her skin.

Tourists filled the boardwalk, and the scent of popcorn, pretzels, and cotton candy floated in the air along with the aroma of the ocean. The Ferris wheel turned in the distance, and cheerful carnival music sounds made everything around her seem happy and carefree.

Everything seemed normal.

Unsettlingly normal.

But she knew things were far from normal.

All these people were continuing about their day, oblivious of the danger they could be facing.

And Cassidy had to make some major decisions.

She was still officially on the clock, but she'd wanted

to talk to Ty for a few minutes. A lot was going on, and they needed to discuss some things.

Especially since three more graves had been dug up today.

Word hadn't yet spread on the island about it because this particular cemetery was off the beaten path, a place most people wouldn't see in passing.

She tried to keep all of it under wraps as much as she could.

But the crime was still equally as disturbing.

Besides that, these graves were newer. They didn't fit Noelle's theory.

Cassidy had no idea what somebody was doing with these bodies, but she didn't like the fact they were stolen. She was still waiting to hear back on the cause of death linked to the bodies in the other graves.

"What do you think is going on?" Ty leaned against the railing and looked out at the ocean.

"I think all of this ties in with Noelle." Cassidy took a sip of her coffee, the vanilla syrup she'd added flooded her tastebuds with a moment of indulgence. "I think I need to call my contact with the FBI. Not because of Noelle necessarily. But these desecrated graves are nothing to be ignored. With summer in full swing, I don't think my officers and I can handle all of this."

"Any news about hiring more officers?"

"The town council gave their preliminary approval. Hopefully, I can begin the hiring process soon."

"That's great news, at least." Ty cast a quick smile as if trying to soften the situation.

Cassidy nodded. "It really is. We're seriously under-staffed. But that will also require building on to the police station. It's just not big enough to accommodate our growth. That means I need to get more approvals."

"I know you guys will figure it all out."

"We will. Eventually." But how much hassle would it all turn into?

She let out a long breath and shifted her thoughts back to Noelle. "What do you know about the Alphas?"

"They're no joke—as Gunner will tell you. There were rumors that the group caught wind the SEALs were coming to execute the rescue and they set his team up."

She straightened as his words settled in her mind. "Wait . . . what sense does that make? Are you saying these Alpha guys knew the SEALs were coming to do a rescue and ambushed them?"

Ty offered a tight shrug. "That's what some people think."

Cassidy shook her head as she tried to comprehend that. "It still doesn't make sense. They abduct three scientists, kill the rest of them. Then they ask for a ransom, kill one of the people they abducted, and eventually bomb their own building. And why kill Thomas Black now?"

Ty motioned for her to keep her voice low. "Maybe they're trying to cover something up. Maybe they haven't given up yet. In the meantime, they decided to wreak some havoc. Maybe to keep Noelle in line."

"I can't help but think there's more to it."

"You could be right. I can tell you this—these guys are pure evil. I don't even want to speak of some of the things they did to people who betrayed them. It involved invoking as much pain as possible."

"And these people could be on the island?"

Ty frowned. "It's a possibility."

"I don't like this, Ty."

"I don't either."

Cassidy's phone rang, and she pulled her thoughts from the conversation.

It was Leggott, one of her officers.

She put the phone to her ear as she answered. "Chief . . . we've got a report on two men on the island who are acting like they've lost their minds."

"Lost their minds?"

"They're raging and trashing their rental house. And they're naked. Bradshaw and Dillinger are dealing with two different car accidents right now and can't get to them. It's more than a one-person call."

"I'll be right there."

Leggott rattled off the address, then Cassidy slid her phone back into her pocket.

The last time she heard about something like this happening on the island was when a deadly gang from the West Coast had invaded Lantern Beach. They'd begun selling something called flakka, a synthetic street drug that was a psychoactive mix of alpha-PVP. It made people act crazy—paranoid, delusional, agitated. Those who took it lost their minds and almost behaved like zombies.

What was happening now?

Cassidy was about to find out.

CHAPTER
TWENTY-SEVEN

GUNNER STARED AT THE PICTURE, his gut tightening at the sight of the man.

"You recognize him?" Noelle asked, studying his expression as if she feared she might miss something.

"He's one of the Alphas."

"What?" Her voice came out wispy.

"His name is Ivan Teranski. Sounds very Russian, doesn't it?"

She nodded as she stared in the distance. "It does. But why would he stop by the office?"

"My guess is that he knew you weren't there. He wanted to send you a message. To shake you up."

She shivered. "It worked."

Gunner felt just as uneasy as Noelle.

How would they stop these guys?

He didn't know. But he didn't like the possibilities in his mind. He needed to call Cassidy and tell her about the photo—as well as send her the image.

With Noelle's permission, he did just that.

When he finished, Noelle turned toward him as they sat in his Jeep. "Is there anything else you can remember from the mission? I was largely in the dark about most of it. I hadn't even heard of the Alphas when they abducted me."

He searched his thoughts for anything that might help. "I was kept in the dark about a lot of things also. I was only told what I needed to know for the mission itself and nothing else."

That was the way it worked. He didn't ask questions. He did what he was told. But the whole situation had felt off for some reason.

"Maybe if we put our heads together, we can get a better picture of what we're up against here." Noelle's gaze implored him to help.

"We both know what we're up against. The Alphas. Look at what they've already done to you."

She rubbed her jaw and cringed.

It had to still be tender from the attack in her home.

"But what exactly are they planning?" Noelle asked.

"It sounds like they're planning on somehow trying to make a super bug version of smallpox that they can spread throughout the United States to destroy us."

"And they needed to dig up those specific bodies on Lantern Beach?" Tension stretched through her voice. "Or were they just random?"

"The Alphas work strategically. There has to be a particular reason. Maybe those are people who died from smallpox."

"But of all the places they could've chosen, why here on Lantern Beach?" she continued.

He ran a hand over his beard, smoothing it. "Maybe because you're here. If they truly are trying to make some type of super bug, then maybe they still need your expertise. Isn't that why they abducted you in the first place?"

Her stomach knotted. "Yes. I guess that theory makes sense."

He turned toward her. "There's one thing I know for sure. If these guys are operating on this island, then we need to find them and stop them."

"You're right. We do. And I have a feeling that's easier said than done." Her frown said it all.

They were in the middle of an impossible situation . . . one that would require everything they had in them.

———

Noelle and Gunner started down the road.

She didn't want to go back to Ty and Cassidy's place. Not yet.

She also had no desire to go back to her house right now either.

Gunner had said he would drive her wherever she wanted. She intended on taking him up on that offer.

"Keep going straight." Noelle pointed to the road ahead.

He cast her a skeptical glance. "You know there's not much down this way, right?"

"I know. Just trust me. You'll see."

Gunner didn't ask any more questions, which she appreciated.

Less than a mile later, she pointed to the entrance to Lantern Beach Community Church. "Here."

He did a double take at her, as if surprised she wanted to go to church.

She shrugged as if sensing his question. "Church is the one place I always feel I can clear my thoughts. Church and the beach, and right now I feel too exposed on the beach."

"Very well." Gunner pulled into a parking space, and Noelle opened the door. Together, they walked toward the church entrance.

"Are you allowed just to go in here?" Gunner asked, pausing near the heavy wooden doors.

"They have times that the sanctuary is open during the day. I do it all the time. I talked to Pastor Jack about it, and he said he was fine with it."

They stepped inside the mostly dark building. Only a few dim lights in the front of the sanctuary were on, and fading sunlight filtered through frosted windows.

Noelle walked toward the front and slid onto the second pew. Gunner slipped in beside her, and they stared together at the cross at the front of the building.

"My faith is really what helped me to heal the most," she started. "Before I was abducted, I wasn't even a believer."

"Really?"

"I'd always relied on what I could see or touch.

What I could explain scientifically. But . . . you gave me that cross when you rescued me," she started. "I found so much comfort in it. And when I got back to the States, I decided to go to church. It was the best thing I could have done, and it was in part thanks to you."

"That's good that you found a place to heal."

She glanced at Gunner. "How about you? You were here on Sunday. What's your story?"

His jaw tightened, and she had the feeling he didn't want to answer.

But she waited anyway, just in case.

"I'm the opposite of you," he finally said. "I was a pretty strong believer until . . ."

"You lost your leg," she finished.

He rubbed his jaw and nodded stiffly. "That changed everything."

"I know it must have been incredibly difficult. Did you blame God for it?"

"Who else is there to blame?"

"How about the people responsible? The Alphas?"

His expression clouded. "God allowed the Alphas to do what they did."

"God allows us all to make our own choices, each with their own consequences. Sometimes those consequences affect other people negatively. But if He didn't give us those choices, then we'd simply be robots, wouldn't we?"

"You make it sound simple." His voice came out as a rumble. "You and Ty both."

"I'm not trying to say that faith and believing in God

is simple. And I know that the issues are far more complicated than that. But I also know that believing in God and in a greater purpose for our lives can put things into perspective and give a lot of clarity. And I think we all need that in life."

"You're right. We do." Gunner stared at the cross.

She decided to continue. "I've learned the hard way that sometimes we have to lose part of ourselves in order to gain something. We have to find a purpose for our pain."

"You speak as if you know."

Noelle swallowed hard as she considered what to say. "I used to be married."

"I didn't realize that." His eyes widened.

She nodded, her throat still tight. "Josh and I had been married two years when our little girl was born."

"You have a daughter?"

Her heart let out a pang as memories overcame her. She'd thought it would get easier to talk about, but it hadn't.

Tears pressed at her eyes as grief fell on her like a curtain.

"Betsy is in heaven now." Her voice sounded strained as she said the words. "She had Scalded Skin Syndrome."

"Noelle . . . I had no idea." His words caught. "I'm so sorry. I can't even imagine . . ."

"We tried everything we could to save her. But in some cases, the syndrome can be fatal."

"To say that sounds difficult sounds like such an

understatement. That explains why you specialize in what you do."

She nodded, more moisture filling her gaze. "I want to help other people so they don't have to go through what I did."

"That also put a huge strain on your marriage, didn't it?"

She forged ahead, knowing if she stopped now, she wouldn't be able to continue. "Our marriage didn't survive the loss. It's not actually that uncommon, unfortunately. I dealt with my grief by working endless hours. Josh dealt with his grief by cheating on me."

Gunner shifted, locking his gaze on hers. "That's horrible."

"It's not something I like to talk about." Noelle drew in a deep breath. "So I may not have lost a leg, but I do understand a little about losing things that are important to you."

Gunner grabbed her hand and squeezed it.

Warmth flooded her veins at his touch.

He continued holding her hand as they both stared at the cross again.

Noelle wished she could read Gunner's thoughts. But she didn't ask what he was thinking.

Instead, she sat for several more minutes and looked at the cross, lifting silent prayers. Prayers for wisdom. For strength. For safety for her and those around her.

But her blissful moment was interrupted when she heard something rustling at the back of the church.

Someone else was here with them, she realized.

CHAPTER
TWENTY-EIGHT

GUNNER HEARD the noise and rose.

He glanced at the back of the church but didn't see anything.

Was someone else here?

"Stay here," he mumbled.

Then he strode toward the back of the church.

Withdrawing his gun, he opened the swinging doors leading into the lobby area.

It was dark out here.

There were tables and a wooden stairway on one side.

Was someone hiding there?

Everything was quiet around him.

Of course, this could be anyone. Not necessarily one of the Alphas.

He couldn't let this situation mess with his judgement.

"Hello?" he called.

No answer.

Another sign that if someone was here they didn't have good intentions

He looked around the lobby.

No one was here.

But he'd definitely heard someone.

Alarm filled him when he thought of Noelle. What if this was a scheme to separate them?

He rushed back into the sanctuary.

As soon as he saw Noelle and that she was okay, relief filled him.

But the look on her face said something more had happened.

"Noelle?" He walked closer.

She held up her phone. "I just got another message —it says, 'We need you. Soon.'"

His gut tightened. He didn't like this.

"Let's get out of here," he murmured as he took her arm.

He checked his Jeep as they climbed inside. Checked everything around him.

He didn't see anyone.

But someone had been in the church with them. He was certain of it.

They took off down the road.

Gunner kept thinking about that conversation with Noelle. It had been unexpected.

When he reflected on what she'd shared about her loss, his level of respect for her only grew.

She'd also been through an unimaginable hurt.

You have to give purpose to your pain.

That was what Noelle had said.

She was right. Unless a person found meaning in the hard times in life, then bitterness and resentment could kick in.

Gunner had certainly been there before. Had certainly struggled with those things.

But he felt something changing inside him, something he'd been fighting a long time.

God had brought him here for a purpose.

Yes, God.

Gunner had been rebelling against all thoughts of faith, feeling as if God had let him down.

Going to church was one of the last places he'd expected Noelle to ask him to go.

He wanted to deny that what she'd said about God made sense.

But he couldn't do that. Because Noelle was right.

God had been there with him all along. Gunner was the one who'd pulled away.

When they arrived at Ty and Cassidy's place, Gunner and Noelle climbed out of the Jeep. Kujo met them in the driveway, and Gunner rubbed the dog's head.

Another moment of longing filled him.

Longing for a family of his own. A house to come home to. Even a dog to greet him.

He'd thought that kind of life wasn't for him. That his future couldn't hold those things.

But what if he'd been wrong?

It was growing darker outside. It had been a long day, and it wasn't over yet.

———

Noelle and Gunner had just walked in the house when Cassidy drove up and followed them inside.

She told them about the two men on the island who were acting crazy.

Noelle sank onto the couch a little harder than she intended as she processed what Cassidy had told her. "Two different people on the island have the same symptoms? Symptoms of being unbalanced?"

Cassidy nodded grimly as she lowered herself into the chair across from her. "They're at the clinic right now being tested. I thought it was a drug overdose at first, but after seeing how they were acting I'm not certain."

"Did they have any type of rash?" Noelle asked.

"I didn't notice anything."

Noelle chewed on the side of her lip before saying, "When I talked about the Alphas releasing some type of biological warfare, I assumed it would be a variant of smallpox. What if it's something completely different? Something that affects somebody's brain chemistry?"

Cassidy narrowed her eyes as she observed her. "Then why do they want to involve you if that's the case? That's not your specialty."

Adrenaline still pulsed through Noelle as her

thoughts raced. "I don't know. I don't really have any good guesses right now. But I'd like to see these people. Talk to them. Is that possible? Could I go to the clinic?"

Cassidy remained stoic a moment before nodding. "I don't see why not. I'll have to talk to Doc Clemson once we get there. But you certainly have enough degrees to examine these people for yourself if need be."

Gunner rose. "I'd like to go also. Right now, I don't want Noelle out of my sight."

Something about his words caused Noelle's face to heat.

She knew he only said that to be practical, and she understood.

But it had been a long time since anyone had gone out of their way to protect her. Usually she was the one in charge. The leader.

It felt good to know someone had her back as well.

"We need to make sure that no one else with any other symptoms has come in." Noelle rose, anxious to see these people for herself. "Any strange symptoms at all. We need to look for a pattern until we know what exactly is going on with all of this."

"Do you think we should call the CDC?" Cassidy asked.

Noelle thought about it a moment. "Let me go to the clinic first and see these people with my own eyes. What we don't want is to pull the trigger prematurely, especially if it turns out to be nothing. I should know more once I see them."

Cassidy rose also. "Okay then. Let's go."

Noelle hoped for answers—but she also hoped her gut feeling was wrong.

TWENTY-NINE

AS CASSIDY HEADED down the road, she mentally ran through apprehending those two men earlier today.

It was just as Leggott had reported—they were acting like they were out of their minds. They'd been climbing on the side of the rental house—on the outside of the exterior stairway—when Cassidy arrived. It had been quite the ordeal to get them down.

Even when they'd gotten the men down, they'd still thrashed around, seeming abnormally strong. Their pupils had been dilated and their words slurred.

It had been a long time since Cassidy had seen anything like that.

She wanted to believe they'd taken some sort of drug that had caused them to act that way.

But what if it was more than that?

What if the Alphas had something to do with this?

It was too early to know. Doc Clemson was doing bloodwork on them. Hopefully when they had those results, they'd have more answers.

But a bad feeling brewed inside her.

She was anxious to hear what Noelle thought about the men, who'd since been subdued. But they still weren't acting normal.

Noelle was clearly smart. Most likely, she was far more qualified to diagnose something like this than Doc Clemson would be. Doc Clemson was a good doctor, but he didn't have a specialty in infectious diseases.

Cassidy's mind rushed through various scenarios as she headed down the road. How would she handle an outbreak on the island?

No one would be able to leave. They'd all be stuck here together, cut off from land . . . and possibly from help.

Her stomach twisted into knots at the thought.

Quickly, she dialed Mac MacArthur's number. He was the mayor and the former police chief as well as a friend and mentor.

When he answered, Cassidy gave him a quick recap on what was going on. If trouble of this magnitude had come to the island, he needed to know. They'd need to develop some type of plan if that were the case.

"I don't like the sound of this, Cassidy." Concern stretched through Mac's voice, just as she'd expected.

"Believe me, I don't either. I hope to have some more answers soon."

"Let me know when you do."

"I will," she promised.

Finally, Cassidy pulled up to the clinic. She waited for Gunner and Noelle to park beside her, and then they all walked in together.

But somehow, Cassidy felt as if she were walking onto a minefield.

———

Noelle paused at the entrance of the clinic and braced herself for whatever she might find inside.

"Do you think we need to put on hazmat suits?" Cassidy turned toward her, questions glimmering in her gaze. "To quarantine anyone?"

Noelle thought about it a moment before shaking her head. "Not yet. We don't have enough information. But it is a good idea to isolate the two men you brought in earlier."

"I'll talk to Doc Clemson and give him the update. You wait in the hallway for now, okay?"

Noelle nodded as a thrum of nerves raced through her.

She had trained for this. At one point in her life, she'd thought this was what she wanted to do.

But after what happened to her daughter, she'd changed her mind. Then after her abduction, she began working for Ocean Essence. They'd given her permission to work on products geared toward the pharmaceutical skincare market, to help issues such as the one her daughter had dealt with.

However, Noelle had now been thrust back into this position.

As she stared at the wall, her heart pumping out of control, Gunner squeezed her arm and brought her back to reality.

She cast him a glance, hoping to show her gratitude for his support.

"You'll do great," he murmured reassuringly.

"Thanks." She cast a fleeting glance his way, careful not to look at him for too long. He might see all the self-doubt in her gaze if she did.

She didn't want to make the wrong call on this.

The implications . . . they could be far-reaching. Bigger than her and the people around her. Bigger than this island.

But she couldn't proclaim the sky was falling either. She needed to remain level-headed.

Finally, Cassidy emerged from Doc's office and motioned for Noelle to join them.

"I'll keep a lookout out here." Gunner planted himself against the wall.

"Good idea. Thanks."

Noelle slipped inside Doc Clemson's office and lowered herself into the seat across from him. Another flutter of nerves rushed through her. "Thank you for letting me be a part of this. What's going on with these two guys who were brought in?"

"Dr. Purdy . . ." He got right to the point, any of his

usual humor gone. "The patients are displaying confusion and agitation. Their heartrate is elevated. Cognitive function has declined."

"Are these symptoms getting better or worse?"

"They seem to be leveling off some now that they're being treated here at the clinic." He propped his elbows on his desk and leaned closer. "Does this sound like symptoms of any condition you're familiar with?"

Noelle let out a soft breath. "It's hard to say. Most conditions I've seen don't have psychotic effects. Where would they have picked this up if it's a virus?"

"Without further data, we don't have the answer to that."

"We've feared for a long time that terrorists could target the water system in our country," Cassidy reminded them. "Is that a possibility?"

Noelle didn't like the thought of that, though she had heard the theory thrown out before. "If that's the case, everyone's at serious risk. How much longer until the blood tests come back?"

"We're looking at least a couple of hours for the more advanced tests. The initial blood panel should be back any time now."

Noelle had expected that. "I'd really like to see these patients myself. Do you think that's possible? I know I don't have a license to practice medicine in North Carolina. But I'd like to talk to them in more of a research capacity if that's okay."

Clemson slowly nodded. "I think we can make it work."

Noelle stood, knowing there was no time to waste. She needed to see these guys and determine if whatever was wrong with them was in any way contagious.

Her gaze locked with Doc Clemson's. "I'm ready when you are."

CHAPTER
THIRTY

"HAVE you noticed any other patterns in the patients who are coming in?" Noelle asked Doc Clemson as they headed down the hallway at the clinic toward the first patient's room. "I know it's tourist season so you're going to be getting a lot of people who aren't regulars."

"I haven't noticed anything yet," he told her. "But now that I'm aware of the situation, I'll definitely keep my eyes open. In the meantime, Dr. Mercer and I will peruse the most recent reports we've written up on patients to make sure we haven't missed anything."

Noelle nodded. "That's a good idea. Also, if you can check in with the clinics in surrounding counties, we can see if they've seen cases like this."

"Of course. I'll just have to get the patients' permission. I don't think that will be a problem."

While Noelle waited near the examination rooms, she gave Gunner a nod to let him know everything was okay—so far.

A few minutes later Doc gave her the okay to go in.

She stepped into the first patient's room—Michael Morrison—and asked for permission to look at his medical records. He agreed.

"Mr. Morrison." She paused by the bedside of the twentysomething man with blond hair. His arms were restrained on the hospital bed until he calmed down. "How are you feeling?"

"Great." He slurred the word, and his eyes looked glazed as his head wobbled up toward her.

Noelle checked his vitals. Observed his skin for any lesions. Looked at his pupils.

She saw no signs of anything biological. Most likely, this was simply drugs.

Her heart calmed ever so slightly.

Hopefully, the blood tests would be ready earlier than expected. Clemson had put a rush on them.

She asked Michael a few more questions, but his responses weren't particularly useful. He was too out of it to be of much help.

A knock sounded at the door, and a sun-kissed blonde stepped inside and introduced herself as his girlfriend.

The woman's eyes were swollen and red with tears. "Is he going to be okay?"

"I hope so," Noelle answered honestly. "Did anything unusual happen today before he started acting strange?"

She shook her head. "No, not really. Everything was normal. We were getting ready to go to the beach. Right before we left, he started talking nonsense and acting as if he didn't know who I was."

"But nothing triggered it? There was nothing odd about today?"

She shook her head again. "Not that I can think of. We had lunch—sandwiches and chips, the same stuff we've been eating all week. Then we put on our sunscreen, grabbed our towels, packed some drinks in a cooler, and started outside. That's when Michael went crazy."

"I've got to get away from the ants!" Michael's head shot up, and he began screaming in fear. "The ants are everywhere! Get them off me!"

He thrashed around as panic consumed him.

Noelle sucked in a breath as she watched him.

What in the world was going on?

———

Gunner felt himself bristle when he saw someone familiar step through the main entrance of the clinic.

Rex Houghton.

What was that man doing here? Had he followed Noelle? Was he that desperate to coerce her into a date?

Rex paused in front of Gunner and narrowed his eyes. "What are *you* doing here?"

"I was about to ask you the same." Gunner bristled at the man's tone.

"That's none of your business."

"You brought it up," Gunner reminded him.

Rex scowled and looked away. "Do you know where I check in?"

Gunner nodded toward a desk manned by a nurse in the distance. "Right over there."

So Rex was at the clinic to be checked out. That was interesting.

Gunner didn't see any obvious signs something was wrong with him. But that didn't mean anything.

Several minutes later, he crept closer as a nurse led Rex into the triage area. It was only closed off by a curtain so much of the conversation could be overheard.

"A few hours ago, I began to develop these bumps on my palms," Rex said. "I'm not sure what they are. They're not painful, just a little itchy."

Gunner's heart raced. Bumps on his palms?

He didn't know much about smallpox. But wasn't that one of the symptoms?

He needed to let Noelle know.

Now.

"BUMPS ON HIS HANDS?" Noelle repeated as she stared up at Gunner in the hallway.

She'd just finished examining the second man who'd had a mental break, and he appeared to be in the same state as the first. He was delusional and strong. He didn't mutter anything about ants. Instead, he'd wanted to climb high enough to reach the sun.

Their delusions didn't make much sense—then again, most people's didn't.

Gunner nodded and reminded Noelle to lower her voice, which had climbed higher with her question. "I didn't see the bumps, but I overheard Rex telling a nurse about them."

"Show me where you last saw him."

Wasting no more time, Gunner led her down the hallway. Rex was out of triage and sitting back in one of the many seats in the waiting room.

As soon as Rex saw her, he stood. A charming smile

stretched across his face. "Noelle . . ."

"We need to get you into a room." She glanced behind her and saw Doc Clemson heading her way.

She motioned to him, then whispered an explanation of the situation. Alarm spread across his face, and he indicated for them to follow him.

Then he led Noelle and Rex to an empty examination room and asked Rex to sit down.

After casting them suspicious glances, Rex lowered himself on the side of the bed.

"Can somebody tell me what's going on here? Why are you here at the clinic, Noelle?" He looked perturbed, with his narrowed eyes and brisk manners. He was no doubt annoyed that they weren't explaining every detail to him.

"I'll explain later. Right now, I need you to turn your hands over." Noelle didn't care if he was annoyed or not. Hurting his pride was the least of her concerns.

He sighed. "Fine. But I don't see what the big deal is. Contact dermatitis, right?"

"We need to be the judge of that." She studied the red blisters popping up on his palms.

A bad feeling jostled inside her.

"Do you have these bumps anywhere else?" She stared into his blue eyes as she waited for his answer.

"I don't know. This is the only place I've noticed them."

"I need to see your back."

He stared at her, an uneasy look in his eyes. "What's going on?"

"I'll explain later. Right now, I need to see your back."

He gave her another lingering scowl before tugging his shirt off. "Fine."

But as Noelle examined the rest of his skin, she didn't see any other indications of smallpox. Some of the tension eased from between her shoulders.

"Do you have a fever?" She placed her hand on his forehead.

He felt cold to the touch.

"The nurse didn't say anything when she took my temperature." He narrowed his eyes as he tugged his shirt back down. "Why?"

"Sore throat? A cough? Congestion?"

"No to all of those." The sharp edge returned to his voice. "Now somebody tell me what's going on!"

Noelle exchanged a glance with Doc Clemson.

The last thing they needed was for information like this to get out. The possibility of a deadly disease being unleashed would send everyone on the island into a panic.

"It could be shingles," she finally said, knowing her words could be true. "Whenever we see a rash like this, we need to rule certain things out."

Rex stared at her, making it clear he didn't fully buy her explanation. "You seem awfully alarmed for it to be shingles."

"We're just being cautious." She stepped toward the door, wanting to run a few things past Doc Clemson in private. "For now, stay here."

Rex's expression shifted from irritated to almost playful, almost as if he'd rethought his approach. "I kind of like it when you're bossy."

Noelle ignored the statement and stepped away.

The next instant, his eyes rolled back.

He began convulsing.

Clemson rushed toward him and turned the man on his side as two nurses darted in.

He glanced at one of his nurses. "Get the anti-seizure medicine."

She hurried from the room.

As Doc Clemson took over, Noelle stepped out of their way.

She lifted a prayer as it seemed everything was spinning out of control.

Gunner felt a rush of apprehension when he saw Noelle head toward him, a new urgency in her gaze.

She'd been in that room with Rex for over an hour. He'd seen the nurses rush inside with medical equipment he couldn't identify.

He'd felt the urgency in the air.

Noelle looked exhausted. Circles were beginning to appear under her eyes, and her skin looked pale. As her makeup wore off, more of the bruises and cuts from her earlier attack were exposed.

Everything that had happened was taking a toll on her.

"Is Rex okay?" Gunner asked as she paused in front of him.

"We ran into a . . . a complication. For now, we're trying to get this situation under control. The CDC is on the way so they can check him out."

"The CDC? Are they sure it's not poison oak? Or an allergic reaction?"

More weariness stained her gaze. "We don't know for sure. For now, Doc's just being extra cautious. He doesn't want to overlook anything."

That was only smart.

"What about the other men?" Gunner asked. "Did you find out anything from them?"

"Not yet. Their bloodwork should tell us a lot. But we're still waiting on some more definitive tests."

He studied her face a moment, sensing she was feeling overwhelmed.

That's when he nodded toward a door in the distance. "You want to step away for a moment?"

"That sounds nice."

They slipped into a small chapel at the back of the clinic and closed the door. Two stained-glass windows with lights behind them adorned the walls. Three small wooden pews and a small platform with an open Bible filled the space. The dim lighting in the room was a refreshing change from the harsh lights of the clinic.

Gunner turned toward her and swallowed hard as he tried to form his next words. "Listen, I want to say that I'm sorry I accused you of having nefarious intentions on Sunday."

Noelle tilted her head to the side. "It's okay if you were suspicious. Anyone in your shoes would be."

His thoughts raced through what he would like to say. There was so much.

But for the first time in a long time, he'd found himself praying.

Really praying.

And really wanting to believe that God existed and that He cared.

Because He did.

And Gunner had always known that. Sure, maybe he'd been upset with God for everything that had happened. But Gunner had always known that God was real.

Everything that Noelle had told him at the church earlier rang true.

He did need a purpose for his pain.

He could turn this tragedy into triumph.

Gunner mentally chided himself for sounding like a self-help book.

But all those statements were true. He was only sorry it had taken him this long to realize it.

His attention went back to Noelle as she ran a hand through her hair.

Then she looked up at him, something close to despair in her gaze. "This could be a catastrophe, Gunner."

He reached for her and squeezed her hand. "Let's pray it's not."

AS NOELLE'S gaze stopped on Gunner, her heart throbbed in her chest.

In just a short period of time, he'd gone from someone who'd only existed in her dreams and memories to someone tangible, someone who'd appeared in her real life.

He was broken but healing.

And her feelings for the man had only grown stronger.

Except that he was no longer a believer.

But he *had* just said something about prayer. Had the mention of it just been something he said in passing but hadn't really meant?

"Noelle . . ." He swallowed hard. "I ran away from God, and it was a terrible mistake."

It was almost as if he'd read her mind.

"It was a mistake?" Noelle repeated, wanting to

make sure she understood correctly what he was saying.

"I know we've talked about resurrecting the dead virus. But what if we could talk about resurrecting a soul that was dead?"

A flash of warmth filled her chest at his words, at the implications of what he was saying. "There's a lot to be said about resurrecting things. About stirring up ghosts from the past and slaying them. Then starting new again. I've certainly been there before, and all things are possible."

They shared a smile.

But Noelle's grin quickly disappeared. "I'm worried about my mom."

He squeezed her arm. "I know. I wish I could take some of those fears away."

"If you said you could, I know you'd be lying. And I appreciate you not lying to me." She swallowed hard. "Have you heard anything about the team Ty put together to find her?"

"They had a lead they were working on. That was the last thing I heard. Ty and his guys are good. If anyone can find her, it's them."

"I hope so."

As a tear rolled down Noelle's face, Gunner pulled her into his arms.

She didn't fight it.

Instead, she buried herself in his embrace, relishing the comfort of his strength.

She wished she could stay like this forever. That she could forget everything going on.

But there was no use pretending.

That wasn't reality.

She had a lot of work in front of her, and she couldn't afford to waste any time.

Noelle pulled out of Gunner's embrace.

She froze when she realized their faces were mere inches apart. As she gazed into his warm brown eyes, she recognized just how much Gunner had come to mean to her.

Noelle had known from the moment they first met that there was something magnetic about him—about the two of them together. This week had only confirmed it.

Before she could overthink things, Noelle leaned toward him and pressed her lips against his.

She wasn't sure where the inclination had come from. She wasn't normally the type to be so forward.

But she'd been wanting to kiss Gunner for a long time.

Now, she'd acted on it. Maybe it was the crazy situation they were in. Maybe she'd realized how short time was. Maybe it was her heightened emotions or the fact that they weren't promised tomorrow.

She waited to see how Gunner would respond.

He remained stiff only a moment before returning the kiss—a long, slow kiss that made her toes tingle.

For a moment, Noelle forgot her problems, and everything else around her seemed to fade away.

If only that feeling could last forever.

———

Gunner felt absolute bliss wash over him.

Noelle had kissed him.

Beautiful, brilliant Noelle.

The woman who could have stepped out of his dreams. Who marked off everything on his mental list of his ideal woman. She was God-fearing, smart, humble, and she made his heart race.

Now she was here in his arms.

He couldn't believe it.

Then the reality of the situation hit him.

He couldn't take advantage of her right now while she was in such an emotional state. That wasn't the way he operated.

But he'd gotten caught up in the moment and—

He pulled away from her, suddenly ashamed of himself.

Maybe a little too abruptly.

"I'm sorry," he murmured.

Noelle reeled as if shocked, almost as if she'd been slapped. "You're sorry?"

Her statement sounded more like a question as she stared at him.

That hadn't come out right, he realized.

He shifted, ignoring the urge to move closer to her. "Noelle . . . I shouldn't have let that happen. You're vulnerable right now, and that's—"

"Wait, you shouldn't have kissed me back because I'm vulnerable?"

"You're in a tough place, and I don't want to take advantage of you . . ."

Realization raced through her gaze, and her lips tugged up in a slow smile. "I think I understand."

"Good." Relief washed through him.

"But I'm a thirty-two-year-old woman who's capable of standing on my own feet. I've loved and lost. I've grieved. I've been through the fire. And you are in no way taking advantage of me right now. It's a sweet thought, though."

His eyes widened. "Oh, I—"

Before he could finish his statement, Noelle leaned forward and pressed another kiss into his lips.

This time, Gunner didn't resist. Instead, he loosened and leaned into her, his lips exploring hers.

There was so much more he wanted to know.

But when he heard footsteps in the hallway, he pulled away.

Noelle gave him one last smile before she turned to see who was at the door.

Cassidy stuck her head inside the room. "Hey, I was looking for you. The CDC just landed. They should be here any minute now. I thought you'd like to know."

The CDC?

Things were about to get real.

And everyone needed to give their full attention to the situation.

Especially Noelle.

CHAPTER
THIRTY-THREE

NOELLE COULDN'T STOP THINKING about the kiss.

But she had to shift her thoughts.

Officials from the CDC were here.

She needed to tell them what she knew.

There was much more at stake here right now than her heart.

It was also her future, and the future of everyone around her.

Noelle stepped into Doc Clemson's office, where she was introduced to Drs. Marv Blanco and Susan Wiseman.

She shared with them what she believed was going on.

"The disease has been eradicated," Dr. Wiseman, a brunette in her fifties, crossed her arms, not bothering to hide the skepticism from her voice.

"I realize that. But I have it on good authority that

the Alphas may have resurrected it to use to infect people now." Noelle stared at them as she waited for her words to settle.

Dr. Blanco still looked dumbfounded as he stared at her. "Do you realize how many millions of people died from smallpox?"

She nodded. "I do."

"I don't like the sound of this." He let out a sigh. "We'd like to see these patients ourselves."

"Of course."

They all stepped out of the office. Clemson showed them to Rex's room first.

As Noelle waited outside, she spotted Gunner and Cassidy talking in a hallway in the distance.

She decided not to interrupt them and wandered toward the lobby instead. She wanted to see if anyone else had come in with symptoms they should be concerned about.

The waiting room was surprisingly empty.

That was good news.

Strange diseases and symptoms weren't spreading like wildfire.

As she paused near the nurse's station, a dark-haired man in his forties approached her.

"Excuse me . . . I'm Harry, a friend of Rex's," he started. "A colleague, actually. I heard he came into the clinic. How is he?"

A colleague? Maybe he could answer some questions about Rex.

"I think he's doing fine." Doc Clemson had given

her a quick update in his office with the CDC present. Rex was lucid and stable at the moment. "Do you mind if I ask you a few questions."

He narrowed his eyes with curiosity. "Go ahead. What do you need to know?"

Noelle crossed her arms, trying to remain calm. "When was the last time you saw Rex?"

"This morning. We had breakfast together to talk about a project we're working on for one of Rex's companies."

"I see. Did he seem normal?"

"He seemed like himself." Harry shrugged.

"Did he eat anything unusual?"

Harry thought about her question a moment before shaking his head. "Not to my knowledge. I mean, I think he got a shrimp and avocado breakfast burrito with some fruit on the side. Didn't seem like anything too out of the ordinary in my opinion."

Noelle nibbled on her bottom lip a moment before shaking her head. "No, it doesn't sound like that would cause a problem, as long as he isn't suddenly allergic to shellfish."

"Should I be concerned?"

She considered how to answer. "We're running some tests on him, so we'll know more soon."

"That's good. I hope he's okay."

"Me too." She might not like the man, but she didn't want any harm to come to him. Plus, there were the greater implications of his possible sickness—implications that could affect everyone around them.

"By the way . . ." Harry stood directly in front of her and locked his gaze with hers. "*Vperyod.*"

As soon as Noelle heard the word, her mind reeled back in time.

Spun into a darker place.

A place where helplessness and fear consumed her.

And suddenly nothing made sense . . . including her mental compass that guided her every decision.

———

Gunner's phone rang. He glanced at the screen and saw his friend Pete was calling again. He excused himself from his conversation with Cassidy and stepped outside to take the call.

"Do you have an update?" Gunner started, planting himself on the sidewalk and crossing an arm over his chest.

"You could say that. I've been asking around and trying to find out some information for you. From what I've heard, there was someone on the inside who alerted the Alphas your team was coming."

Gunner's stomach tightened until it felt like a boulder in his abdomen. "That means they had time to plan, to coordinate what they would do when we showed up."

Just as he'd suspected.

"That's right," Pete confirmed.

The boulder inside Gunner grew even heavier. "Do you know who it was?"

"I know this isn't what you want to hear. But rumor has it that it was . . . Freeman."

Gunner sucked in a breath. "What? He would never do that! And even if it were true, why is this the first we've heard about it?"

"We didn't have definitive proof, just a few suspicious phone calls."

Freeman? Could Freeman have done this to them? Had he been working with the Alphas?

If so, the Alphas had turned their backs on him and killed him anyway.

That was the way the group operated, so it wouldn't surprise Gunner.

But still . . .

As soon as that call ended, Gunner dialed Commander Ford.

If anyone had answers to his questions, it would be Ford.

But as the phone rang, Gunner spotted someone walking across the parking lot in the distance.

His back stiffened.

Was that . . . Noelle?

Who was that man she was with? And where were they going?

They must have gone out a back entrance.

Gunner couldn't be sure, but he didn't think the guy was from the CDC.

Tension threaded up his spine.

"Noelle!" he called.

But she didn't turn to look at him.

Instead, she kept walking at a steady pace, climbed into an awaiting car, and the vehicle took off.

Something was wrong. He was certain of it.

Gunner reached into his pocket for his keys.

He needed to go after them.

But when he got to his Jeep, he glanced down and saw all four of his tires had been slashed.

CHAPTER
THIRTY-FOUR

FINISH WHAT YOU STARTED.

The phrase echoed again and again in Noelle's mind, almost like a switch had flipped in her brain.

Nothing else mattered except getting to a lab to finish her work.

Her work on . . . smallpox.

But it didn't make sense.

She'd never worked on it.

She'd been kept in a cell while in captivity, not forced to work in a lab.

Reality and memories clashed inside her until a throb began inside her head.

Something was wrong.

She was certain of it.

She just wasn't sure what.

"Good girl," Harry muttered beside her as he escorted her from the clinic. "You just listen to my instructions, and you'll be just fine."

He kept his hand on her arm as he led her to the black sedan as it waited, engine running, with two men in the front seat.

She knew she should turn back. That she should run.

But she couldn't.

Her motions and thoughts almost felt robotic.

Which made no sense.

She pressed her eyes closed as her head throbbed harder.

What was happening to her?

Why wasn't she fighting?

If she got into the car with this man, she'd likely never see Gunner or anyone else ever again.

"Noelle!" a deep voice yelled behind them.

Her breath caught.

Gunner? Was that Gunner?

Her thoughts blurred again as she tried to make sense of things.

She started to turn when Harry squeezed her arm more tightly. "Ignore him."

Noelle kept walking toward the waiting car.

Complying was the best thing she could do right now. She instinctively knew that.

Harry shoved her inside the vehicle, climbed in behind her, and slammed the door. Then the car took off.

Finish what you started.

The phrase continued to echo in her mind.

As the scent of cigars and expensive cologne filled her, more memories rushed back.

Everything from her time in captivity flooded her mind.

Everything.

She had worked in a lab. Why was she just remembering this now?

She'd put in grueling hours.

Bartholomew had extracted DNA from a corpse that had been found in Siberia. A corpse that the Alphas hoped still contained living molecules of smallpox.

Once he'd done what they wanted, they'd killed him.

Then they'd killed Thomas.

They'd kill her next.

Then when Noelle had done all she could and had been expended, these guys would find someone else to carry out their dirty work.

Unless she stopped them.

But how?

Right now, she had no choice but to help them. Because suddenly she felt like she was a stranger living in her own body, someone incapable of making her own decisions. Something almost robotic had kicked in.

What had they done to her?

This wasn't normal.

They'd done something . . . to her brain.

That was it, wasn't it?

She just couldn't remember what.

She found comfort in the fact that the old Noelle still nagged at her subconscious.

But the sound of her own inner voice was so distant that she wasn't sure it would ever reach the surface.

Her temples pounded.

What had they done to her? And how was she going to fight past it?

———

Gunner rushed back inside and hurried down the hallway toward Cassidy.

She was talking to someone else, but this couldn't wait.

Gunner paused beside her, adrenaline pulsing through him. "Noelle just left with a strange man."

Cassidy stopped talking and turned to him, a wrinkle of concern appearing on her brow. "What?"

"I don't know what's going on. But Noelle just left with a man I've never seen before, and she wasn't acting like herself. I was going to follow, but the tires on my Jeep have been slashed. Someone needs to go after them. It's a black Lexus sedan. The plates are . . ." He rattled off the numbers.

"Come on." Cassidy started toward the door. "Maybe you and I can catch him. I'll call in some backup officers just in case."

As they rushed outside, Cassidy radioed her guys to let them know what was going on and to give them the license plate number.

Then Gunner and Cassidy climbed into her SUV and took off.

"Do you have any idea who he was?" Cassidy rushed as she headed through the parking lot.

"I haven't seen the guy before. I have no idea. I thought he was someone with the CDC at first."

"Those two are still inside." Cassidy's jaw tightened. "I don't like this, Gunner."

"I don't like this either." That was the understatement of the year. Had the Alphas finally gotten to Noelle? Right there in the clinic?

How could Gunner have let that happen? He'd tried to keep an eye on her.

He hadn't seen anyone suspicious . . . but that was the way the Alphas operated, wasn't it? Almost as if they were masters at slight-of-hand tricks.

"Which way did they go?" Cassidy paused at the road.

"South."

Cassidy turned on her siren and sped in that direction.

As they drove, Gunner kept his eyes open for the Lexus.

His phone rang, and he saw Dr. Samantha Reynolds was calling him back.

Gunner hesitated, almost ignoring the call. But he decided he should answer. There was more to what was going on with Noelle than met the eye.

He was certain of it.

Maybe Samantha could provide some insight that

would help them right now. He would continue looking for that sedan as he talked.

"You said that a friend of yours might want to talk to me?" Samantha started.

"She's having some memory issues." Gunner surveyed various island streets, looking for any signs of trouble. He saw nothing. Not yet. Only a lot of tourists. "Unfortunately, this isn't a good time to talk. But I think it's possible my friend has amnesia."

"I see. Are there parts of her life she can't remember?"

"Not exactly. I mean, she doesn't realize she can't remember them."

"What?"

Gunner let out a breath, knowing he wasn't making much sense. He wished he had more time to get into this, but he didn't. He would need to be succinct.

"There are things my friend can't remember from the time period when she was abducted," he told Dr. Reynolds. "But she seems to think she remembers everything."

"That's interesting."

"Are there any other explanations besides amnesia?" He stared out the window.

"It's hard to say for sure without talking to her myself. But off the top of my head, she could have selective amnesia. It *is* suspicious that she thinks she remembers everything. Usually people with amnesia realize there are blocks of time they can't recall."

"So there are other explanations?"

Samantha let out a sigh before saying, "Honestly . . . you know what that sounds like to me?"

He scanned each street as they passed. "What's that?"

"This might sound crazy, but have you ever considered that maybe she was . . . hypnotized."

THIRTY-FIVE

THE MAN in the front passenger seat of the car turned toward her, a cigar in his hand.

A familiar face stared back at Noelle.

Ivan Teranski.

She'd recognize that craggy face and thick blond hair anywhere.

"Good to see you again, Noelle," he said in a strong Russian accent. His gold front tooth glinted in the sunlight.

"It's been a long time." Noelle's voice wavered with instinctive fear. "Where are we going?"

"Somewhere safe. Somewhere you can finish what you started for us."

Noelle squeezed her eyes shut as she struggled to make sense of her thoughts. Her inner battle made her head continually pound.

"But it's been two years." Her throat ached as she said the words. "Why wait so long?"

"Some of our research was destroyed when the building blew up. But we were able to find someone else to complete some work for us for a time. Now you need to complete the rest. This is what you do best. If anyone can complete what we've started, it's you."

So these guys hadn't figured out how to totally recreate the virus. That was good news. But they must be getting close.

"You do know these things aren't something that can be done overnight," she started. "It takes time to grow the samples and test them, to—"

"Thomas already did that, and then he was no longer useful to us." Ivan's lip twitched as he stared back at her. "We're missing the final puzzle piece. That's what we need you for."

Alarm washed through her. They'd killed him after they got what they wanted.

That's what they'd do to her also.

Noelle swallowed hard as her mind raced. How was she going to get out of this situation? She had no idea.

She was a scientist, not a soldier.

Right now, the best thing she could do was to keep gleaning information. Then she could make a rational decision after gathering all the facts.

"So you're almost done?" she clarified as island streets blurred past.

"That's right." He glared at her. "But we're also going to need protection against this virus so we will be unharmed after it is unleashed."

"You mean a vaccination?" More facts clicked in

place. "Again, in the amount of time it takes for testing these things—"

"We don't have time!" His voice rose. "We're already two years behind schedule. Can't you understand that?"

Noelle's thoughts raced. "Why did you dig up those graves?"

He smirked and glanced at the man sitting beside her before shrugging. "We have our reasons."

Her jaw clenched as she tried to imagine what those reasons might possibly be.

They weren't heading toward the ferry dock. How did they plan on getting her off this island? Or did they have a lab set up here?

She found that hard to believe.

Finally, they pulled to a stop near the lighthouse beach.

Noelle saw a helicopter waiting there.

The door opened, and the man who'd beaten her peered out, a scornful look in his eyes. Even though he'd worn a mask before, she was certain it was the same man.

"This time, Anton won't fail." Disdain dripping through Ivan's voice.

Fear swept through Noelle until her head spun.

If she didn't do what they wanted, she would pay the price.

The price being suffering through a slow and painful death.

———

Cassidy screeched to a halt at the lighthouse. She looked up in time to see a helicopter go airborne.

"Oh, no, they didn't," she muttered as she stared at it from behind the driver's seat.

Gunner climbed out of the SUV and glared. "Yes. Yes, they did. How are we going to catch that?"

"I'm going to call in additional backup." Cassidy grabbed her phone. "It's the only choice we have at this point."

"Cassidy . . ." His voice contained grave warning.

She already had her phone to her ear. "I know. Believe me. I know."

A moment later, she ended the call and turned back to Gunner with a frown. "The FBI are at least an hour out."

"We don't have an hour!" Gunner ran a hand over his face.

"I know. But that's what they said. The island is so isolated it takes time to get here."

"That's not going to work."

Cassidy gripped the phone—maybe too hard. There had to be *something* else they could do. She hated the helpless feeling that wanted to consume her.

"Noelle is wearing that tracker I gave her." Gunner climbed back into the SUV. "Wherever they take her, we should be able to find her."

"That's right!" A moment of relief flooded her.

At least they had that.

That was when another idea hit her.

Ty and his guys had worked another mission recently where they'd met a helicopter pilot named Nate "Ghost" Casper. Ghost said he could be here if they needed him. Even though he was based in Arizona, he flew all over. And he had connections.

What were the chances that he might be close and available now? Or that he knew someone who might be?

"I'm going to call Commander Ford," Gunner announced. "Maybe he can help."

"You do that," Cassidy murmured. "I'm going to try someone else. We can't take any option off the table right now."

AN HOUR LATER, the helicopter landed on an old ship in the middle of the ocean in international waters. That's what Noelle had heard Ivan say, at least.

Old World War II era artillery guarded the deck, and the gray paint appeared faded, even in the dark.

Nausea gurgled inside Noelle.

Finish what you started.

The phrase kept echoing in her mind.

Why did she keep thinking that? She wanted to get the thought out of her mind. But it wouldn't leave.

Almost as if the thought had been implanted inside her.

What sense did that make?

She couldn't finish what she started.

But you must.

No, I won't! Her hands fisted at her sides.

The mental battle continued. They must have done

something to her . . . erased part of her memories only to bring them back at their beck and call.

Had they used some type of . . . mind control?

The theory sounded crazy.

But it was the only thing that made sense.

And the Russians . . . they were known for using less traditional methods to get what they wanted.

It fit, didn't it?

Not only that, but it was the only explanation that fit these circumstances.

Her door opened, and Pantyhose Face jerked her out. She'd heard his name earlier. Anton.

This time, she could fully see his face—unlike on the helicopter where a headset had obscured it.

He was in his thirties, with strong features and smooth skin. To look at him, no one would suspect the evil that lurked inside.

"So we meet again," he muttered. "My men are giving me grief for botching things with you earlier. I can't allow that to happen again."

His fingers dug into Noelle's arm until she let out a cry.

But it didn't matter. His grip didn't loosen.

"Where are we going?" Noelle rushed as he began dragging her away from the copter into the bowels of the ship.

"You'll see." He led her through a doorway, down a hallway, and down two sets of stairs.

Finally, Anton opened a locked door and shoved her

inside a cold room that smelled vaguely of metal, grease, and a mix of chemicals.

No one else was inside.

But the bright lights above her were nearly blinding, as were the clean white walls.

Her heart beat harder, so loud it was nearly all she could hear as she studied the space and realized exactly what she was looking at.

The Alphas had set up another state-of-the-art lab here on this old ship.

They'd probably done this just for her.

Or had Thomas been forced to work here too?

All so these men could finish recreating this virus and unleash their evil on the world.

Noelle swallowed the lump in her throat.

She couldn't do what they wanted.

Despite that, she found herself walking toward a microscope.

Again, it almost felt as if someone else were controlling her thoughts and actions. This was what they'd planned, wasn't it?

Terror filled her veins.

———

Ghost was working in California, but he had a pilot friend in Raleigh who'd agreed to help them.

Deacon Compton arrived on the island at the Blackout headquarters about twenty minutes after Cassidy called. Commander Ford had helped Gunner and Ty coordinate their next plan of action. As military contractors, Ford had sanctioned their help.

Though Ford was sending a team to meet them, Ty had already put his own team together. Ty, Colton Locke, Brandon Hale, and Rocco Foster.

"I want to come with you." Gunner stepped forward as the chopper whirled in the distance.

He wouldn't be able to forgive himself if something happened to Noelle. He was willing to do whatever it took to make sure she was safe.

And to make sure this virus wasn't unleashed.

Ty stared at him a moment before nodding. "I think you're ready for this. Let's go."

"Be careful," Cassidy gave her husband a quick kiss. As she did, her radio crackled, and her face went pale.

"What is it?" Ty asked.

"Those bodies that were dug up . . . they're turning up on the island."

"What?"

"We're still investigating. But there was one at Noelle's place. One at Blackout. Another at Mac's. I think they're a scare tactic. Or maybe a distraction. I'm not sure yet."

"I don't like the sound of that."

"But it fits what the Alphas are known for. They're dramatic."

"You can say that again."

"I'll take care of this," Cassidy murmured. "You take care of Noelle . . . and whatever else it is these guys are planning."

The Alphas were leaving dead bodies around the island? Gunner mused.

It sounded like something they would do—just to mess with people's minds.

Just like they'd messed with Noelle's mind.

He felt certain that was what had happened. Why hadn't they seen this earlier?

Gunner climbed into the chopper along with the others.

As they swooshed into the air, he thought about his missing limb.

He prayed his disability wouldn't hold him back.

Then he remembered his renewed faith. His resurrected hope.

He had to believe right now that God was in control.

And he prayed that God would give him the strength to win this battle—not for his own sake.

But for everyone else's.

CHAPTER
THIRTY-SEVEN

"YOU NEED TO WORK FASTER," Anton growled as he lingered behind her, gun in hand as he barked his orders.

The test tube trembled in Noelle's hand. "I've only been here for fifteen minutes. How fast do you expect me to work?"

"I'll do the talking here," the man snapped. "You just work."

Images of his fists slamming into her face flashed back to Noelle, and she cringed with each memory.

This man wouldn't hesitate to hurt her—and she had a feeling the beating he'd given her before was nothing compared to what he could do. Now, he had something to prove.

His ego had been injured when Noelle had thwarted his plans earlier.

Noelle stared at the equipment in front of her and

tried to remain calm. "I need to familiarize myself with what's already been done."

"All the notes are right there from the last guy." He pointed to a leather-bound notebook on the counter near the microscopes.

Had Thomas left these?

Another lump formed in her throat.

She studied the notes a moment, trying to figure out what he'd done.

Then she began looking at samples under the microscope.

More memories from her time in captivity hit her.

Those men had forced Noelle to try to propagate this virus. She'd worked day in and day out.

They'd killed Bartholomew right in front of her.

They would have done the same to her once she gave them what they wanted, but she'd been rescued first.

It seemed they'd known the attack was coming.

They'd planned for it.

Another recollection returned.

A man Noelle had never seen had knelt in front of her. He'd told her people were coming to rescue her. Then he'd done something with his fingers as he moved them in front of her. Something almost like hypnosis.

He'd told her she would forget everything that had happened.

Noelle could only remember being in that room and nothing else unless he'd said *vperyod.*

When she heard that phrase, she would remember

everything and finish what she started. Nothing would stop her. Everything depended on her compliance.

She couldn't complete this task.

Even if it meant certain death.

She glanced at her tormentor and dreaded what that might mean.

She couldn't let her courage fail her . . . no matter what happened.

———

"I see the ship about two miles from here," Deacon said into their headsets. "How close do you want me to get?"

"I need you to stop here," Ty said from the front seat. "We need to get out and approach the boat by water."

Gunner listened to everything, his thoughts racing.

Noelle's tracker had led them here.

He was so thankful they'd thought to put it on her.

He was also thankful that the darkness had fallen. That would make their surprise attack a little easier.

But they didn't know exactly what they were getting into.

Still, even though Noelle probably couldn't develop a virus in a few hours, it would only take moments for these men to kill her if they wanted to.

Anger burned through him at the thought.

Gunner could *not* let that happen.

Colton opened a door, and wind swept inside.

A moment later, he pushed out an inflatable raft with a small engine on the back. The watercraft expanded before hitting the water.

Ty turned toward the rest of the guys. "You know what to do. Let's go."

They'd discussed the plan on the way there. The rest of the team would take Ivan and his men out. While they did that, Gunner would find Noelle.

Quickly, they each climbed down the rope and onto the boat.

Gunner was thankful for the obstacle courses Ty had made him do. Right now, they were proving helpful. He wouldn't have been able to climb down that rope without having trained first.

But he'd done it.

His prosthetic was still in place.

Maybe Gunner wasn't whole in a traditional sense. But he was still capable. He'd simply needed to believe that himself. He'd needed to find the motivation. And he had.

Now he was ready for action.

Rocco started the engine, and the team headed toward the haunting old ship on the horizon.

When they got closer, they cut the engine and paddled the rest of the way to the vessel so they wouldn't alert anyone of their presence.

All was quiet around them except for the waves crashing into the side of the boat.

Brandon threw a rope, and the claw on the end secured it to a railing above.

Then they each climbed aboard the ship.

Gunner gripped his gun as they spread out.

No one was immediately within eyesight on the deck.

But they'd still need to be very careful.

At least they had the element of surprise on their side right now.

As Gunner rounded the corner, someone yelled.

A gunman appeared in front of him.

The man he'd seen escorting Noelle to that vehicle at the clinic.

Fury raced through him, but he held it at bay.

Gunner calmly pulled the trigger.

The bullet hit the man's shoulder, and he fell to the deck.

More yells sounded behind him.

Within seconds a full-on battle had ensued.

While the rest of the team held the men off, Gunner had to find Noelle . . . before she got caught in the crossfire.

CHAPTER
THIRTY-EIGHT

NOELLE'S HANDS trembled as she stared at the microscope in front of her.

"What you're planning on doing is terrible," she finally said. "Why would you want to kill thousands of people?"

"To eliminate the weak, of course." Anton stepped closer.

The hair on her neck rose as she felt his body heat near her.

"The company you work for is just as evil," he muttered. "Don't fool yourself or act so self-righteous."

"What does that mean?" She turned toward him. "They're a cosmetic company."

He smirked. "You really don't know?"

"Know what?" What was he talking about? Was he trying to mess with her head?

Before he could answer, commotion sounded in the distance.

She froze.

What was going on out there? Had help come?

"I don't know what's going on out on the deck, but if you don't finish this, we *will* infect you with the disease ourselves so you can die a slow, painful death," Anton growled. "Do you understand me?"

Her throat tightened at the thought. "I do."

Just then, the commotion became louder as more men yelled. Bullets fired.

Anton bristled, suddenly unable to ignore it. "Stay here. I need to check on those imbeciles."

Gun in hand, he walked to the hatch and opened it. Looked both ways.

While he was distracted, Noelle glanced around the lab.

There was no way she would just stand here and do nothing.

She needed a way to defend herself.

Then she spotted something she could use.

She grabbed a vial and shoved it in the pocket of her lab coat.

A moment later, Anton returned, an urgent look in his eyes. "I don't know what's going on. But we need to move. Now."

He grabbed her arm, and Noelle yelped with pain.

He only gripped harder and tugged her toward the door.

But she had a secret weapon.

The vial . . . which was full of acid.

Should she use it now?

Or would a better opportunity present itself?

She didn't know. But she had to be ready for anything.

She gripped the vial with her free hand.

Could she use it without harming herself? She thought she could.

Before she could ruminate on it any longer, someone stepped into the doorway.

Her breath caught.

Was that . . . Gunner?

It couldn't be . . .

But it was.

He was here.

Her heart flooded with relief.

But Noelle knew this was far from over.

———

Just as Gunner reached the doorway, his gaze stopped on . . . the lab.

Then Noelle.

The man gripping her arm swung his gun toward Gunner.

In the blink of an eye, he fired.

The bullet hit Gunner, and pain shot through him.

He sagged against the wall at the impact.

"No!" Noelle started toward him.

The man yanked her back.

Gunner reached forward, desperate to help.

Before he could, Noelle pulled a vial out of her

pocket, twisted the top off, and flung the liquid inside it at the man's face.

Direct hit.

The man howled with pain, twisting and turning with agony as he released Noelle and held his hands to his face.

Noelle darted past the man toward Gunner and grabbed his arm. "Are you okay? Were you hit?"

Her gaze zeroed in on the bullet hole in his leg.

He touched his pants. "Saved by the prosthetic. I had phantom pain when it happened. It's . . . it's hard to explain. But it took me a moment to realize that also."

Visible relief washed over her. "Of course. I'm so glad you're here."

Gunner grabbed her hand and led her up the stairway. "Stay close to me."

He'd found her, but that didn't mean they were out of trouble yet.

As they reached the deck, a figure stepped out from behind the artillery.

Gunner would recognize the man anywhere.

Ivan Teranski.

The leader of the Alphas.

And the reason Gunner had lost his leg.

"Get behind me," Gunner muttered.

Before Noelle could protest, he shoved her behind him.

"Well, well, well." Ivan stepped closer, his gold tooth glinting in the moonlight and a mocking expression on his face. "I guess we couldn't slow you down after all."

Gunner glanced behind the man and saw Ty.

Ty gave him a thumbs up.

He knew what that meant.

In the distance, a helicopter chopped through the air.

Deacon was on his way to pick them up.

That must mean that Ivan was the only one left. That had been their plan. To only call Deacon when it was time to leave.

"You're not going to stop us, you know." Ivan practically spit out the words, his Russian accent growing even stronger.

"Are you sure about that?" Gunner asked as Deacon's copter came into view.

But before the aircraft reached the ship, another copter swooped in front of it.

A Black Hawk.

The military.

They had arrived.

The pilot steadied the aircraft beside the ship.

Then someone onboard fired.

Ivan started to turn. To yell.

Then he grasped his chest.

A pool of red spread there.

He collapsed to the deck.

Relief swept through Gunner when Ty ran and grabbed the man's weapon.

Ty checked the pulse at the man's neck. Then Ty shook his head. "He's dead."

Ivan was no longer a threat.

One well-placed shot, and the man was dead.

And Noelle was safe.

For now.

But they still needed to get her off this boat.

He'd let the military figure out what to do with the lab below deck.

AS NOELLE STEPPED off the helicopter and back onto Lantern Beach, an immense sense of relief filled her.

The past twenty-four hours had been spent being debriefed by the military and other government officials at a military base in Norfolk.

The rest of the team who'd been sent to rescue her had also been questioned.

Thankfully, the Alphas had been taken out.

Those who hadn't been killed had been arrested.

The government had obtained any samples from the lab.

Based on what Noelle could tell from her time in the makeshift laboratory, what the Alphas had created so far wasn't a threat to mankind.

She was so thankful for that. Because this situation could have turned out so much worse.

However, there were still some loose ends to tie up.

Including her mother.

A frown tugged at Noelle's lips.

Last she'd heard, Ty's guys were close to finding her mom. But she didn't have confirmation yet. If they did find her, Noelle didn't know what kind of state she'd be in.

She continued to pray for the best.

Axel, a Blackout member, waited near an SUV to take her to the police station.

She waved at him and then glanced in the air.

Another helicopter moved in and landed beside the one she'd arrived in.

Her heart leapt into her throat when Gunner emerged and headed toward her.

Relief flooded her.

She'd seen him at the base, but the two of them hadn't had a chance to talk alone. She'd been anxious to be able to do so.

She turned toward Axel and raised her voice to be heard over the helicopter. "Could we have a moment before we leave?"

Axel's eyes sparkled. "Of course."

As soon as Gunner was close enough, Noelle threw her arms around him.

He held her equally as tight, his arms constricting as if he didn't want to let go.

She didn't want to let him go either.

"I'm so glad that you're okay," Gunner murmured in her ear.

"Me too. Thank you for coming for me."

"I'll always come for you."

Noelle's heart nearly beat out of control at his words. She knew without a doubt that they were true. Gunner was a man of character. Their connection undeniable.

She was so thankful God had allowed their paths to cross again.

Gunner leaned toward her and planted a kiss on her lips.

She didn't argue—not even when he drew her closer and deepened the kiss. In fact, she relished every moment.

Until someone cleared his throat behind them.

"I hate to cut this short, but Cassidy is waiting for you down at the police station," Axel said. "She just texted me again."

She and Gunner pulled away and exchanged a giddy smile.

Then hand in hand, they climbed into the awaiting vehicle.

Now, they needed to talk to Cassidy.

———

"These men were more brilliant than I want to admit," Cassidy said as she stared at Noelle and Gunner in her office.

She wouldn't be getting any arguments from Noelle. "Yes, they were. I'm thankful they truly seem to have been stopped this time."

"We're all grateful for that," Cassidy said.

Noelle shifted in her seat. "I haven't heard any updates about the island. How are things here?"

"It's been an interesting twenty-four hours." Cassidy raised her eyebrows. "As you may have heard, the Alphas had some of their men leave dead bodies exhumed from local graves at key locations around the island—locations where they could send a clear message."

Noelle sucked in a breath. No, she hadn't heard.

"What?" Her voice lilted. "Why would they do that?"

"Because what they do best is playing mind games, it appears." Cassidy pressed her lips together, a dry expression to her voice.

Noelle didn't hide her frown. "I can't deny that. They hypnotized me so they could 'reactivate' my thoughts later."

"I know." Gunner scowled and squeezed her hand more tightly. "That explains all the gaps in what had happened. That and the fact that Freeman sold us out. The Alphas knew they had to preserve their work, so they made sure you temporarily forgot about it. Then they blew up the lab to destroy any evidence and killed two of my men. I was supposed to die also."

Noelle's heart squeezed with grief at the thought of what could have happened.

There was already so much loss . . . but she was thankful there would be no more.

"Apparently, the Alphas got hold of those two guys

who were acting crazy and did some type of hypnosis on them as well," Cassidy continued. "Again, they just wanted to distract us from the real issues that were going on so they could get ahold of you."

"And it worked." Noelle squeezed Gunner's hand again. "Just not the way they wanted it to."

"We're thankful for that," Gunner murmured.

Noelle shifted as she continued to try to collect her thoughts. "What about Rex? The bumps on his hands and his seizure?"

"Doc Clemson thinks it was caused by an autoimmune reaction," Cassidy said. "We're still waiting to hear for sure, but he'd been having unusual responses to several different foods—though he didn't want to admit it. Certain foods could have caused both the rash and the seizure. But his bloodwork didn't show any viruses."

"That's good." Some of the air left her lungs as relief filled her.

"It looks like maybe we can finally put this behind us." Cassidy offered a long, slow nod as if she were trying to wrap her mind around that idea also.

"Bury it where it deserves to be buried." Gunner gave them both a pointed look. "In the past."

Cassidy raised her eyebrows. "Exactly. I'm just thankful that everyone is safe. Thank you two for your help with that."

The three of them chatted a few more minutes until finally Noelle and Gunner stood. But before they went out the door, Cassidy called Gunner's name.

"I just happen to be hiring some more officers here on the island. Are you interested?"

His eyes widened, and then he glanced down at his leg. "Even with . . ."

"I haven't seen any instances where your prosthetic has held you back. I think you can handle it."

Noelle's gaze connected with his. "I think you can too."

Gunner remained expressionless for a moment until finally a small smile tugged at the side of his lips. "I'm going to have to think about that offer. But I have to say that, off the top of my head, it sounds too good to pass up."

Cassidy grinned. "I was hoping that that was what you would say. I'll give you a couple of days, and then I'll ask you again. How about that?"

"That sounds perfect."

Noelle and Gunner left the police station hand in hand.

Gunner staying on the island?

That was an idea she could get used to.

But something Anton said lingered in her mind.

He'd mentioned that Ocean Essence was just as evil as the Alphas. What had he meant by that? The troubles at the company were over, right?

She nibbled on her bottom lip.

She'd have to think about that more later. Most likely, he was just trying to play more mind games with her.

Just as she and Gunner stepped outside, a car pulled to a stop in the parking lot.

Noelle braced herself, halfway expecting the worst.

Who could blame her after everything that had happened?

It would probably be a long while before she would stop being hypervigilant.

Gunner tugged her back, obviously apprehensive also.

The back door opened and . . . Noelle's mother stepped out.

Tears flooded Noelle's eyes at the sight of her. She hadn't expected to hear anything yet.

Now, here her mom was. Her clothes were clean, her hair styled, and makeup adorned her face.

Noelle dropped Gunner's hand and ran to meet her. Noelle threw her arms around her mother, thankful her mom looked healthy and unharmed.

Noelle was so grateful to see her . . . even if her mom couldn't remember who she was.

Her mother pulled away and studied Noelle's face a moment until recognition flashed in her gaze.

"Noelle?" Her voice sounded scratchy as the name left her lips.

More tears rushed to Noelle's eyes. "Yes, it's me, Momma."

She knew her mom might not remember for long . . . maybe not even for more than a few seconds.

But Noelle was grateful for this moment.

So, so grateful.

"Momma, this is Gunner." Noelle stepped back.

Her mom took his hand. "I can see my daughter is very much in love with you."

Noelle flushed, but she didn't deny her mom's words. Even in her sickness, her mother could see the truth, couldn't she?

Noelle had been in love with Gunner for a long time.

It was like Gunner had said.

Noelle couldn't wait to put the past behind her. To bury it.

Instead, she wanted to explore the wonderful possibilities of the future.

A future here on Lantern Beach . . . with her mom.

And, from the sounds of it, with Gunner also.

~~~

Thank you for reading **Troubled Graves**. If you enjoyed this book, please consider leaving a review.

Coming next: **Deceptive Shallows**.
~~~

USA TODAY BESTSELLING AUTHOR
CHRISTY BARRITT
DECEPTIVE
SHALLOWS

ALSO BY CHRISTY BARRITT:

OTHER BOOKS IN THE LANTERN BEACH SERIES:

LANTERN BEACH MYSTERIES

Hidden Currents

You can take the detective out of the investigation, but you can't take the investigator out of the detective. A notorious gang puts a bounty on Detective Lady Matthews's head after she takes down their leader, leaving her no choice but to hide until she can testify at trial. But her temporary home across the country on a remote North Carolina island isn't as peaceful as she initially thinks. Living under the new identity of Cassidy Livingston, she struggles to keep her investigative skills tucked away, especially after a body washes ashore. When local police bungle the murder investigation, she can't resist stepping in. But Cassidy is supposed to be keeping a low profile. One wrong move could lead to both her discovery and her demise. Can she bring justice to the island . . . or will the hidden currents surrounding her pull her under for good?

Flood Watch

The tide is high, and so is the danger on Lantern Beach. Still in hiding after infiltrating a dangerous gang, Cassidy Livingston just has to make it a few more months before she can testify at trial and resume her old life. But trouble keeps finding her, and Cassidy is pulled into a local investigation after a man mysteriously disappears from the island she now calls home. A recurring nightmare from her time undercover only muddies things, as does a visit from the parents of her handsome ex-Navy SEAL neighbor. When a friend's life is threatened, Cassidy must make choices that put her on the verge of blowing her cover. With a flood watch on her emotions and her life in a tangle, will Cassidy find the truth? Or will her past finally drown her?

Storm Surge

A storm is brewing hundreds of miles away, but its effects are devastating even from afar. Laid-back, loose, and light: that's Cassidy Livingston's new motto. But when a makeshift boat with a bloody cloth inside washes ashore near her oceanfront home, her detective instincts shift into gear . . . again. Seeking clues isn't the only thing on her mind—romance is heating up with next-door neighbor and former Navy SEAL Ty Chambers as well. Her heart wants the love and stability she's longed for her entire life. But her hidden identity only leads to a tidal wave of turbulence. As more answers emerge about the boat, the danger around her rises, creating a treacherous swell that threatens to reveal her past. Can Cassidy mind her own business, or will the storm surge of violence and corruption that has washed ashore on Lantern Beach leave her life in wreckage?

Dangerous Waters

Danger lurks on the horizon, leaving only two choices: find shelter or flee. Cassidy Livingston's new identity has begun to feel as comfortable as her favorite sweater. She's been tucked away on Lantern Beach for weeks, waiting to testify against a deadly gang, and is settling in to a new life she wants to last forever. When she thinks she spots someone malevolent from her past, panic swells inside her. If an enemy has found her, Cassidy won't be the only one who's a target. Everyone she's come to love will also be at risk. Dangerous waters threaten to pull her into an overpowering chasm she may never escape. Can Cassidy survive what lies ahead? Or has the tide fatally turned against her?

Perilous Riptide

Just when the current seems safer, an unseen danger emerges and threatens to destroy everything. When Cassidy Livingston finds a journal hidden deep in the recesses of her ice cream truck, her curiosity kicks into high gear. Islanders suspect that Elsa, the journal's owner, didn't die accidentally. Her final entry indicates their suspicions might be correct and that what Elsa observed on her final night may have led to her demise. Against the advice of Ty Chambers, her former Navy SEAL boyfriend, Cassidy taps into her detective skills and hunts for answers. But her search only leads to a skeletal body and trouble for both of them. As helplessness threatens to drown her, Cassidy is desperate to turn back time. Can Cassidy find what she needs to navigate the perilous situation? Or will the riptide surrounding her threaten everyone and everything Cassidy loves?

Deadly Undertow

The current's fatal pull is powerful, but so is one detective's will to live. When someone from Cassidy Livingston's past shows up on Lantern Beach and warns her of impending peril, opposing currents collide, threatening to drag her under. Running would be easy. But leaving would break her heart. Cassidy must decipher between the truth and lies, between reality and deception. Even more importantly, she must decide whom to trust and whom to fear. Her life depends on it. As danger rises and answers surface, everything Cassidy thought she knew is tested. In order to survive, Cassidy must take drastic measures and end the battle against the ruthless gang DH-7 once and for all. But if her final mission fails, the consequences will be as deadly as the raging undertow.

LANTERN BEACH ROMANTIC SUSPENSE

Tides of Deception

Change has come to Lantern Beach: a new police chief, a new season, and . . . a new romance? Austin Brooks has loved Skye Lavinia from the moment they met, but the walls she keeps around her seem impenetrable. Skye knows Austin is the best thing to ever happen to her. Yet she also knows that if he learns the truth about her past, he'd be a fool not to run. A chance encounter brings secrets bubbling to the surface, and danger soon follows. Are the life-threatening events plaguing them really accidents . . . or is someone trying to send a deadly message? With the tides on Lantern Beach come deception and lies. One question remains—who will be swept away as the water shifts? And will it bring the end for Austin and Skye, or merely the beginning?

Shadow of Intrigue

For her entire life, Lisa Garth has felt like a supporting character in the drama of life. The designation never bothered her—until now. Lantern Beach, where she's settled and runs a popular restaurant, has boarded up for the season. The slower pace leaves her with too much time alone. Braden Dillinger came to Lantern Beach to try to heal. The former Special Forces officer returned from battle with invisible scars and diminished hope. But his recovery is hampered by the fact that an unknown enemy is trying to kill him. From the moment Lisa and Braden meet, danger ignites around them, and both are drawn into a web of intrigue that turns their lives upside down. As shadows creep in, will Lisa and Braden be able to shine a light on the peril around them? Or will the encroaching darkness turn their worst nightmares into reality?

Storm of Doubt

A pastor who's lost faith in God. A romance writer who's lost faith in love. A faceless man with a deadly obsession. Nothing has felt right in Pastor Jack Wilson's world since his wife died two years ago. He hoped coming to Lantern Beach might help soothe the ragged edges of his soul. Instead, he feels more alone than ever. Novelist Juliette Grace came to the island to hide away. Though her professional life has never been better, her personal life has imploded. Her husband left her and a stalker's threats have grown more and more dangerous. When Jack saves Juliette from an attack, he sees the terror in her gaze and knows he must protect her. But when danger strikes again, will Jack be able to keep her safe? Or will the approaching storm prove too strong to withstand?

Winds of Danger

Wes O'Neill is perfectly content to hang with his friends and enjoy island life on Lantern Beach. Something begins to change inside him when Paige Henderson sweeps into his life. But the beautiful newcomer is hiding painful secrets beneath her cheerful facade. Police dispatcher Paige Henderson came to Lantern Beach riddled with guilt and uncertainties after the fallout of a bad relationship. When she meets Wes, she begins to open up to the possibility of love again. But there's something Wes isn't telling her—something that could change everything. As the winds shift, doubts seep into Paige's mind. Can Paige and Wes trust each other, even as the currents work against them? Or is trouble from the past too much to overcome?

Rains of Remorse

A stranger invades her home, leaving Rebecca Jarvis terrified. Above all, she must protect the baby growing inside her. Since her estranged husband died suspiciously six months earlier, Rebecca has been determined to depend on no one but herself. Her chivalrous new neighbor appears to be an answer to prayer. But who is Levi Stoneman really? Rebecca wants to believe he can help her, but she can't ignore her instincts. As danger closes in, both Rebecca and Levi must figure out whom they can trust. With Rebecca's baby coming soon, there's no time to waste. Can the truth prevail . . . or will remorse overpower the best of intentions?

Torrents of Fear

The woman lingering in the crowd can't be Allison . . . can she? Because Allison was pronounced dead six years ago. Musician Carter Denver knows only one person who's capable of helping him find answers: Sadie Thompson, his estranged best friend and someone who also knew Allison. He needs to know if he's losing his mind or if Allison could have survived her car accident. Could Allison really be alive? If so, why is she trying to harm Carter and Sadie? As the two try to find answers, can Sadie keep her feelings for Carter hidden? Could he ever care for her, or is the man of her dreams still in love with the woman now causing his nightmares?

LANTERN BEACH PD

On the Lookout

A runaway woman. A dead body. A mysterious compound. When Cassidy Chambers accepted the job as police chief on Lantern Beach, she knew the island had its secrets. But a suspicious death with potentially far-reaching implications will test all her skills—and threaten to reveal her true identity. Cassidy enlists the help of her husband, former Navy SEAL Ty Chambers. As they dig for answers, both uncover parts of their pasts that are best left buried. Not everything is as it seems, and they must figure out if their John Doe is connected to the secretive group that has moved onto the island. As facts materialize, danger on the island grows. Can Cassidy and Ty discover the truth about the shadowy crimes in their cozy community? Or has darkness permanently invaded their beloved Lantern Beach?

Attempt to Locate

A fun girls' night out turns into a nightmare when armed robbers barge into the store where Cassidy and her friends are shopping. As the situation escalates and the men escape, a massive manhunt launches on Lantern Beach to apprehend the dangerous trio. In the midst of the chaos, a potential foe asks for Cassidy's help. He needs to find his sister who fled from the secretive Gilead's Cove community on the island. But the more Cassidy learns about the seemingly untouchable group, the more her unease grows. The pressure to solve both cases continues to mount. But as the gravity of the situation rises, so does the danger. Cassidy is determined to protect the island and break up the cult . . . but doing so might cost her everything.

First Degree Murder

Police Chief Cassidy Chambers longs for a break from the recent crimes plaguing Lantern Beach. She simply wants to enjoy her friends' upcoming wedding, to prepare for the busy tourist season about to slam the island, and to gather all the dirt she can on the suspicious community that's invaded the town. But trouble explodes on the island, sending residents—including Cassidy—into a squall of uneasiness. Cassidy may have more than one enemy plotting her demise, and the collateral damage seems unthinkable. As the temperature rises, so does the pressure to find answers. Someone is determined that Lantern Beach would be better off without their new police chief. And for Cassidy, one wrong move could mean certain death.

Dead on Arrival

With a highly charged local election consuming the

community, Police Chief Cassidy Chambers braces herself for a challenging day of breaking up petty conflicts and tamping down high emotions. But when widespread food poisoning spreads among potential voters across the island, Cassidy smells something rotten in the air. As Cassidy examines every possibility to uncover what's going on, local enigma Anthony Gilead again comes on her radar. The man is running for mayor and his cult-like following is growing at an alarming rate. Cassidy feels certain he has a spy embedded in her inner circle. The problem is that her pool of suspects gets deeper every day. Can Cassidy get to the bottom of what's eating away at her peaceful island home? Will voters turn out despite the outbreak of illness plaguing their tranquil town? And the even bigger question: Has darkness come to stay on Lantern Beach?

Plan of Action

A missing Navy SEAL. Danger at the boiling point. The ultimate showdown. When Police Chief Cassidy Chambers' husband, Ty, disappears, her world is turned upside down. His truck is discovered with blood inside, crashed in a ditch on Lantern Beach, but he's nowhere to be found. As they launch a manhunt to find him, Cassidy discovers that someone on the island has a deadly obsession with Ty. Meanwhile, Gilead's Cove seems to be imploding. As danger heightens, federal law enforcement officials are called in. The cult's growing threat could lead to the pinnacle standoff of good versus evil. A clear plan of action is needed or the results will be devastating. Will Cassidy find Ty in time, or will she face a gut-wrenching loss? Will Anthony Gilead finally be unmasked for who he really is and be brought to justice? Hundreds of innocent lives are at stake . . . and not everyone will come out alive.

LANTERN BEACH ESCAPE

Afterglow

What if you married someone, only to discover that she was suspected of killing her former fiancé? While on their honeymoon, Grayson and Rachel Stewart are confronted with dark details of Rachel's past. As more facts begin emerging, their new marriage is thrown into a tailspin. The newlyweds must figure out how to move forward . . . and Grayson must figure out if he married a killer.

LANTERN BEACH BLACKOUT

Dark Water

Colton Locke can't forget the black op that went terribly wrong. Desperate for a new start, he moves to Lantern Beach, North Carolina, and forms Blackout, a private security firm. Despite his hero status, he can't erase the mistakes he's made. For the past year, Elise Oliver hasn't been able to shake the feeling that there's more to her husband's death than she was told. When she finds a hidden box of his personal possessions, more questions—and suspicions—arise. The only person she trusts to help her is her husband's best friend, Colton Locke. Someone wants Elise dead. Is it because she knows too much? Or is it to keep her from finding the truth? The Blackout team must uncover dark secrets hiding beneath seemingly still waters. But those very secrets might just tear the team apart.

Safe Harbor

Guilt over past mistakes haunts former Navy SEAL Dez Rodriguez. When he's asked to guard a pop star during a music festival on Lantern Beach, he's all set for what he hopes is a breezy assignment. Bree hasn't found fame to be nearly as fulfilling as she dreamed. Instead, she's more like a carefully crafted character living out a pre-scripted story. When a stalker's threats become deadly, her life—and career—are turned upside down. From the start, Bree sees her temporary body-guard as a player, and Dez sees Bree as a spoiled rich girl. But when they're thrown together in a fight for survival, both must learn to trust. Can Dez protect Bree —and his carefully guarded heart? Or will their safe harbor ultimately become their death trap?

Ripple Effect

Griff McIntyre never expected his ex-wife and three-year-old daughter to come to Lantern Beach. After an abduction attempt, they're desperate for safety. Now Griff's not letting either of them out of his sight. Bethany knows Griff is the only one who can protect them, despite the fact that he broke her heart. But she'll do anything to keep her daughter safe—even if it means playing nicely with a man she can't stand. As peril ripples through their lives, Griff and Bethany must work together to protect their daughter. But an unseen enemy wants something from them . . . and will stop at nothing to get it. When disaster strikes, can Griff keep his family safe? Or will past mistakes bring the ultimate failure?

Rising Tide

Benjamin James knows there's a traitor within his former command. The rest of his team might even think it's him. As danger closes in, he must clear himself and stop a deadly plot by a dangerous terrorist group. All CJ Compton wanted was a new start after her career ended under suspicion. Working as the house manager for private security group Blackout seems perfect. But there's more trouble here than what she left behind. As the tide rushes in, the stakes continue to rise. If the Blackout team fails, it's not just Lantern Beach at stake —it's the whole country. Can Benjamin and CJ over-come their differences and work together to find the truth?

LANTERN BEACH GUARDIANS

Hide and Seek

During a turbulent storm, a child is found on the beach, washed up from the ocean. Making matters worse—the girl can't speak. Lantern Beach Police Chief Cassidy Chambers can feel the danger lurking around them. As more mysterious incidents happen on the island, Cassidy fears each crime is somehow connected to this child—a child no one has reported missing. Cassidy knows the girl's life depends on finding answers. With the help of her husband, Ty, a former Navy SEAL, she scrambles to discover what exactly is going on. Someone appears to be playing a deadly version of hide-and-seek—and using the girl as a pawn. But what will happen when the game finally ends? *Hide and Seek is the first book in a three book series. Though the main storyline of each book will be wrapped up at the end, some plot lines will not be resolved until the end of book three.*

Shock and Awe

They thought the worst was over—but they were wrong.When Police Chief Cassidy Chambers arrives at a grisly crime scene, she's shocked at where the evidence leads. Then the threats start coming. Threats against her. Threats that could upend her life.As more clues are uncovered, a sinister plot is revealed, and Cassidy fears the little girl in her care may be tangled in a deadly scheme. Cassidy and her husband, Ty, will do anything to protect the child, each other, and the island. But what happens when they might not be able to save all three?

Safe and Sound

A call for help draws Police Chief Cassidy Chambers

deep into a wooded, isolated area on Lantern Beach. What she finds shakes her to the core—a friend is bleeding out, and his last words before dying are: They know. Figuring out who killed her friend and what his final words meant becomes Cassidy's mission. Have members of the notorious gang that placed a bounty on her head discovered her new life? Or is someone else trying to teach her a twisted lesson? Elements from past investigations surface and threaten more than one person's safety. Cassidy and her husband, Ty, must make sense of the deadly secrets that unfold at every turn. If not, the life they've built together might come to a permanent end.

LANTERN BEACH BLACKOUT: THE NEW RECRUITS

Rocco

Former Navy SEAL and new Blackout recruit Rocco Foster is on a simple in and out mission. But the operation turns complicated when an unsuspecting woman wanders into the line of fire. Peyton Ellison's life mission is to sprinkle happiness on those around her. When a cupcake delivery turns into a fight for survival, she must trust her rescuer—a handsome stranger—to keep her safe. Rocco is determined to figure out why someone is targeting Peyton. First, he must keep the intriguing woman safe and earn her trust. But threats continue to pummel them as incriminating evidence emerges and pits them against each other. With time running out, the two must set aside both their growing attraction and their doubts about each other in order to work together. But the perilous facts they discover leave them wondering what exactly the truth is . . . and if the truth can be trusted.

Axel

Women are missing. Private security firm Blackout must find them before another victim disappears. Axel Hendrix likes to live on the edge. That's why being a Navy SEAL suited him so well. But after his last mission, he cut his losses and joined Blackout instead. His team's latest case involves an undercover investigation on Lantern Beach. Olivia Rollins came to the island to escape her problems—and danger. When trouble from her past shows up in town, she impulsively blurts she's engaged to Axel, the womanizing man she's seen while waitressing. Now, she may not be the only one in danger. So could Axel. Axel knows Olivia might be his chance to find answers and that acting like her fiancé is the perfect cover for his latest assignment. But he doesn't like throwing Olivia into the middle of such a dangerous situation. Nor is he comfortable with the feelings she stirs inside him. With Olivia's life—as well as both their hearts—on the line, Axel must uncover the truth and stop an evil plan before more lives are destroyed.

Beckett

When the daughter of a federal judge is abducted, private

security firm Blackout must find her. Psychologist Samantha Reynolds doesn't know why someone is targeting her. Even after a risky mission to save her, danger still lingers. She's determined to use her insights into the human mind to help decode the deadly clues being left in the wake of her rescue. Former Navy SEAL Beckett Jones needs to figure out who's responsible for the crimes hounding Sami. He's not sure why he's so protective of the woman he rescued, but he'll do anything to keep her safe—even if it means risking his heart. As the body count rises, there's no room for error. Beckett and Sami must both tear down the careful walls they've built around themselves in order to survive. If they don't figure out who's responsible, the madman will continue his death spree . . . and one of them might be next.

Gabe

When former Navy SEAL and current Blackout operative Gabe Michaels is almost killed in a hit-and-run, the aftermath completely upends his life. He's no longer safe—and he's not the only one. Dr. Autumn Spenser came to Lantern Beach to start fresh. But while treating Gabe after his accident, she senses there's more to what happened to him than meets the eye. When she digs deeper into his past, she never expects to be drawn into a deadly dilemma. Gabe has been infatuated with the pretty doctor since the day they met. Now, can he keep her from harm? Could someone out of his league ever return his feelings or will her past hurts keep them apart? As danger continues to pummel them, Gabe and Autumn are thrown together in a quest to find answers. More important than their growing attraction, they must stay alive long enough to stop the person desperate to destroy them.

LANTERN BEACH MAYDAY

Run Aground

A dead captain on a luxury yacht leads to a tumultuous seafaring journey . . . Med student Kenzie Anderson, tired of letting others chart her future, accepts a job as second steward aboard Almost Paradise. But when she finds the captain dead before the charter even begins, her plans seem to capsize. Jimmy James Gamble senses something vulnerable and slightly naive about Kenzie when he finds her on the docks. Realizing danger may still be lingering close, he uses his hidden skills to earn a place on the charter. But being there causes him to risk everything—especially as more suspicious incidents occur. As they set out to sea, Kenzie and Jimmy James both wonder if they're in over their heads. They must figure out how to stop a killer before anyone onboard is hurt . . . otherwise, both their futures might just run aground.

Dead Reckoning

A yachtie fears for her life when she's the only witness to a murder . . . Kenzie Anderson knows what she saw at the harbor—a woman strangled and pushed overboard. But there's no proof of a crime . . . only her word. Jimmy James Gamble believes Kenzie, even if no one else does. As he senses the danger in the air, all he wants is to keep her away from any more trouble—especially after their last charter. Either Kenzie or the yacht they're working on seem to be a magnet for murder and mayhem. Someone is willing to kill to get what he wants—and will do so again if necessary. Can Jimmy James and Kenzie navigate these unfamiliar waters? Or will relying on dead reckoning lead them to their deaths?

Tipping Point

Awakening in a boat surrounded by nothing but water, a yachtie has no doubt someone wants her dead. Kenzie Anderson is determined not to let anyone scare her away from completing the charter season—even with the threats on her life. The only person she can trust is Captain Jimmy James Gamble, despite their tumultuous relationship. Kenzie and Jimmy James both suspect turbulent currents rush beneath the tranquil surface aboard the luxury yacht Almost Paradise. Secrets seem to abound, each one increasing the tension aboard the boat. As answers rise to the surface, neither Kenzie nor Jimmy James is prepared for what they find. Have they both reached their tipping points? Their adversaries want nothing more than to make Kenzie disappear . . . forever. It may be too late for a mayday call.

LANTERN BEACH CHRISTMAS

Silent Night

Catch up with your favorite Lantern Beach characters as they come together to help the town's beloved police chief. On the night before Christmas Eve, as she begins her maternity leave, Lantern Beach Police Chief Cassidy Chambers disappears. Suspecting foul play, law enforcement officers combine forces with the Blackout Security team and island residents to find her. Despite a snowstorm in his path, Cassidy's husband, Ty, desperately tries to return home in time to save her. With his wife's and baby's lives on the line, he needs a Christmas miracle. Will the tightknit community of Lantern Beach be able to rescue their beloved police chief in time? Or will Cassidy's cries for help be met only with silence?

LANTERN BEACH BLACKOUT: DANGER RISING

Brandon

Physically he's protecting her. But emotionally she's never felt more exposed. The last person tech heiress Finley Cooper ever wanted to see again was Brandon Hale. Two years ago, Brandon shattered her heart. Now Finley needs protection, and, against her wishes, Brandon is assigned the job. Even worse, they must pretend to be a couple in order to find answers. Brandon, a former Navy SEAL, met Finley while on an undercover assignment in Ecuador. But he broke her trust, and now he doesn't blame Finley for hating him. As a new Blackout operative, Brandon's first assignment throws him into Finley's life 24/7. Someone wants her dead, and it's clear this person won't stop until that mission is accomplished. To keep her safe, Brandon must regain Finley's trust. Can he convince her she's more than a job to him? Or will peril permanently silence them?

Dylan

His job is to protect her. The trouble is . . . she doesn't want protection. Former Navy SEAL Dylan Granger's new assignment requires him to use both his tactical abilities and his acting skills. Hired by Katie Logan's father, his job is to protect the gutsy university professor while concealing his identity. To maintain his cover, he takes the unassuming role of her new assistant. Katie—a disgraced reporter—has stumbled upon a lead she can't ignore. Now it's clear someone is targeting her, but she refuses to back down. Her handsome new assistant is a welcome distraction from the chaos. But Dylan's skillset goes way beyond his job description, and Katie begins to suspect there's more to Dylan than he's letting on. Dylan's mission can't be disclosed—not if he wants to keep Katie safe. But as his feelings for her grow and the danger increases, keeping his secret becomes more of a challenge than he ever imagined. With innocent lives on the line, Dylan must choose between protecting Katie or savings others.

Maddox

He's on the case . . . and she's his prime suspect. Classified technology is missing, a delivery driver is dead, and former Navy SEAL Maddox King must find the culprits before a dangerous plan is enacted. To find answers, the Blackout agent must go undercover as a maintenance man at millionaire Seymore Whitlock's estate. While there, he sets his sights on Whitlock's personal assistant, Taryn Parsons, a woman who has everything to gain and nothing to lose. Six months ago, Whitlock plucked Taryn out of obscurity to become his caretaker. But with deadly incidents haunting the estate, Taryn doesn't know who she can trust—including the new maintenance man who is both intriguing . . . and unnerving. The stakes continue to escalate, and Maddox is running out of time to find answers. With the body count rising along with his list of suspects, this assignment may be his most challenging yet . . . for both his skillset and his heart.

Titus

She shattered his heart once. Can he set her betrayal aside for the sake of his country? The last person Titus Armstrong wants to join forces with is the woman who dumped him for his brother, Alex. But Presley Lennox is Blackout's best chance at infiltrating a dangerous organization known as The System and finding out more about their deadly plans. Presley Lennox wants out—of both an abusive relationship and the radical group she's become entangled with because of Alex.

When Titus reappears in her life, he's like an answer to prayer—until he asks her to dive deeper into the very life she's been trying to escape. A dangerous plan is brewing that could destroy thousands of lives. Titus and Presley may be the only ones who can stop what's about to be unleashed. Failure would mean certain chaos . . . not only for them but for their nation.

BEACH BOUND BOOKS AND BEANS MYSTERIES

Bound by Murder

When widow Talitha Robinson buys an old store on the boardwalk in Lantern Beach, North Carolina, she's in for a surprise . . . or several. She plans to renovate the space and open Beach Bound Books and Beans, but never expects to find a decades-old skeleton hidden inside one of the walls. As word of the discovery spreads across the island, strange occurrences begin to occur around her. It soon becomes clear someone still knows something about the dead person—something they don't want discovered. Thankfully, former police chief and current mayor Mac MacArthur seems just as eager to unravel the mystery behind the skeletal remains as Tali. But as the two bind together to solve the case, a devastating secret is revealed. Will their newfound friendship come unglued before they find the answers to the past? Or will their blooming relationship die like the man hidden in the wall?Bound by Murder is book 1 in a four book series of novellas. Though the main mystery is resolved, there are threads that will continue throughout the entire series.

Bound by Disaster

Talitha Robinson is knee-deep in renovations as she prepares to open her new bookstore when a body washes ashore on Lantern Beach. While news of the suspicious death surges across the island, a stranger comes knocking on Tali's door, begging her to endorse his unfinished suspense novel. Unable to dissuade the author, Tali is left holding his manuscript in her hands. But she has no idea of the peril written on its pages. Mac MacArthur has kept his distance from Tali since they uncovered a shocking connection about their pasts. But when someone begins to act out the murderous scenes from the book, one victim at a time, Mac's protective instincts override his decision to stay away. As danger escalates, Mac and Tali must manage their conflicting feelings as they work together to stop this killer . . . before the last chapter is written.

Bound by Mystery

Talitha Robinson is well on her way to completing renovations for her new bookstore, Beach Bound Books and Beans, in Lantern Beach, North Carolina. But when she hosts a friendly meet-and-greet with bookstore owners from nearby islands, the progress she's making comes to a deadly end. Someone is backstabbed—literally—right under Tali's nose. To make matters worse, Tali's fingerprints are all over the murder weapon and a neighbor claims to have seen Tali commit the crime. Mac MacArthur knows Tali isn't the type to hurt anyone, but it doesn't take a former police chief to figure out things don't look good for her. The two work together to read between the lines and decipher the truth before Tali gets locked away for crimes she didn't commit. As more evidence stacks up, it becomes clear that someone wants to take Tali out of the story. For good.

Bound by Trouble

With the grand opening of Beach Bound Books and Beans, Tali Robinson's dreams are finally coming true. She hopes to now put the past behind her and start a new chapter. When a suspicious stranger mysteriously shows up at her celebration, her hopes disappear faster than a bestseller at a book signing.Mac MacArthur is ready to solidify his relationship with Tali. But mending their differences is easier said than done. Then someone sets their sights on Tali—and wants to put her out of print . . . permanently. With trouble brewing, Tali and Mac have no choice but to dive into the chaos of the past. However, as more answers are revealed, the danger increases. The truth will come at a great cost . . . one that will bind them together or drive them apart.

Bound by Mayhem

As cast and crew members prepare for Lantern Beach's first annual Christmas play, catastrophe strikes. Abby Mendez, the director and brainchild behind the play, never shows up for a dress rehearsal. Threats emerge, and it becomes clear that not everyone on the island feels the Christmas spirit. With dangerous encounters and ghostly disappearing acts threatening not only the play but also the safety of Lantern Beach residents, former police chief Mac MacArthur and Abby's friend Tali Robinson jump in to help. The stakes rise as the perpetrator continues to haunt Abby's past, torment her present, and threaten her future. When it seems all hope is nearly lost, can the people of Lantern Beach work together to save the play? Or will this phantom scrooge steal the final act?

FOG LAKE SUSPENSE

Edge of Peril

When evil descends like fog on a mountain community, no one feels safe. After hearing about a string of murders in a Smoky Mountain town, journalist Harper Jennings realizes a startling truth. She knows who may be responsible—the same person who tried to kill her three years ago. Now Harper must convince the cops to believe her before the killer strikes again. Sheriff Luke Wilder returned to his hometown, determined to keep the promise he made to his dying father. The sleepy tourist area with a tragic past hadn't seen a murder in decades—until now. Keeping the community safe seems impossible as darkness edges closer, threatening to consume everything in its path. As The Watcher grows desperate, Harper and Luke must work together in order to defeat him. But the peril around them escalates, making it clear the killer will stop at nothing to get what he wants.

Margin of Error

Some secrets have deadly consequences. Brynlee Parker thought her biggest challenge would be hiking to Dead Man's Bluff and fulfilling her dad's last wishes. She never thought she'd witness two men being viciously murdered while on a mountainous trail. Even worse, the deadly predator is now hunting her. Boone Wilder wants nothing to do with Dead Man's Bluff, not after his wife died there. But he can't seem to mind his own business when a mysterious out-of-towner burst into his camp store in a frenzied panic. Something—or someone—deadly is out there. The killer's hunger for blood seems to be growing at a brutal pace. Can Brynlee and Boone figure out who's behind these murders? Or will the hurts and secrets from their past not allow for even a margin of error?

Brink of Danger

Ansley Wilder has always lived life on the wild side, using thrills to numb the pain from her past and escape her mistakes. But a near-death experience two years ago changed everything. When another incident nearly claims her life, she turns her thrill-seeking ways into a fight for survival. Ryan Philips left Fog Lake to chase adventure far from home. Now he's returned as the new fire chief in town, but the slower paced life he seeks is nowhere to be found. Not only is a wildfire blazing out of control, but a malicious killer known as "The Woodsman" is enacting crimes that appear accidental. Plus, there seems to be a strange connection with these incidents and his best friend's little sister, Ansley Wilder. As a killer watches their every move and the forest fire threatens to destroy their scenic town, both Ryan and Ansley hover on the brink of danger. One wrong move could send them tumbling over the edge . . . permanently.

Line of Duty

Jaxon Wilder didn't plan on returning home to Fog Lake, Tennessee, following his tour of duty in Iraq. But after a gut-wrenching failure during his stint in the Army, he now faces a new challenge: his family. Abby Brennan always did her best to be the good girl and to live by the rules. When a wrong decision changes her entire life, she tries to hide from the world. However, a madman known as the Executioner is determined to find her and enact his own brand of justice. When Jaxon and Abby are thrown together in the killer's crosshairs, they're forced to depend on one another to survive. Will Jaxon's sense of duty be enough to help keep Abby safe? Or will deadly secrets lead to the penalty of death?

Legacy of Lies

The justice system failed her family—and so did her hometown. Madison Colson knows deep down that her father—a convicted serial killer—is innocent. But believing it and proving it are two entirely different things. Unable to help her father, Madison has spent most of her adult life overcompensating by helping others. When her aunt dies unexpectantly, duty calls her back to Fog Lake, Tennessee, a beautiful but painful place she'd rather forget. Terrifying events begin to unfold once she arrives, unleashing her worst nightmares. The Good Samaritan Killer—or a copycat—is back, and now Madison Colson is his target. FBI Special Agent Shane Townsend is determined to stop the deadly rampage that has sent the tightknit community into a frenzy. But he needs to earn Madison's trust first. The task feels impossible, especially considering his father is the one who put her dad in prison. With the whole town on edge and pointing fingers, tension escalates out of control. Madison and Shane must sort the facts from the lies—and fight for a legacy of truth—before The Good Samaritan Killer has the final say.

Secrets of Shame

A killer has a promise to keep . . . Attorney Isaac Colson only wants to put his tumultuous past in Fog Lake behind him and return to his life in Memphis. But when an ominous text threatens that he must come back or there will be deadly consequences, he knows he can't take any chances. Rebecca Moreno has only ever loved one man—her high school sweetheart, Isaac Colson. But when his dad went to prison for murder, Rebecca's father forbade them from seeing each other again. Years later, Isaac is back in town and old feelings are stirring. But Rebecca is harboring a secret that could change everything. When The Good Samaritan Killer strikes again, guilt pummels her. She has to tell Isaac the truth.

But as events unfold, she has more to lose than ever. Isaac and Rebecca must find answers—their lives depend on it. But everyone seems to have secrets, each that forms an obstacle to finding the truth . . . and to staying alive.

Refuge of Redemption

Home is a place of refuge—unless it's a killer's playground. For years, Bear Colson has been known as the serial killer's son. But now, someone else is behind bars for the crimes his father was accused of committing. Bear wants to believe hope for a brighter future is in sight, but he has reason to suspect more than one killer was involved. Forensic photographer Piper Stephens' career crashed and burned when she trusted the wrong man. Now, after discovering an alarming secret about the infamous Good Samaritan Killer, she sets out to find both answers and redemption. But things go awry when her assistant becomes the next victim. As fear batters Fog Lake residents once again, Bear and Piper join forces to track down the truth. But the killer is determined to remain in the shadows—and he'll destroy anyone who stands in his way.

ABOUT THE AUTHOR

USA Today has called Christy Barritt's books "scary, funny, passionate, and quirky."

Christy writes both mystery and romantic suspense novels that are clean with underlying messages of faith. Her books have sold more than four million copies and have won the Daphne du Maurier Award for Excellence in Suspense and Mystery, have been twice nominated for the Romantic Times Reviewers' Choice Award, and have finaled for both a Carol Award and Foreword Magazine's Book of the Year.

She is married to her Prince Charming, a man who thinks she's hilarious—but only when she's not trying to be. Christy is a self-proclaimed klutz, an avid music lover who's known for spontaneously bursting into song, and a road trip aficionado.

When she's not working or spending time with her family, she enjoys singing, playing the guitar, and exploring small, unsuspecting towns where people have no idea how accident-prone she is.

Find Christy online at:

www.christybarritt.com

www.facebook.com/christybarritt

www.twitter.com/cbarritt

Sign up for Christy's newsletter to get information on all of her latest releases here: **www.christybarritt.com/ newsletter-sign-up/**

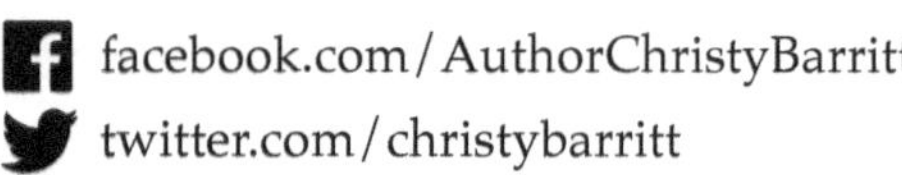